"Hungry?"
She had to raise her voice to be heard over the sound of rushing water.

"Starving, but I really have to be going," he yelled back.

Sure you do. Against her better judgment, she hovered outside the bathroom door. She couldn't resist the urge to go in and talk to him—but he was in the bathroom. He deserved his privacy. And he'd be naked. But what the heck, it was *her* clear shower stall and it wasn't like they'd been playing tiddlywinks all night. She'd seen him as naked as he could get.

She stepped in.

He was wet and golden and amazing, skin glowing as he scrubbed it down under the steaming flow. She was sidetracked for a moment, watching him. Back turned to her, he bent over to soap his feet… oh, my. Whoever said that men were more easily aroused by visual stimuli didn't know what they were talking about. Could any woman ever get tired of such a sight? Then she remembered her purpose for entering. "You're sure I can't offer you anything? Coffee?"

He turned to her, water dripping off his eyelashes and down his lips. "I'd love to, honey, but time's against me."

Books by Simona Taylor

Kimani Romance

Dear Rita
Meet Me in Paris

SIMONA TAYLOR

lives on her native Caribbean island of Trinidad—a fertile place for dreaming up scorching, sun-drenched romance novels. She balances a career in public relations with a family of two small children and one very patient man, while feeding her obsession with writing.

She has also published three works of women's literary fiction under her real name, Roslyn Carrington, but it is her passion for romance that most consumes her. When not dreaming up drool-worthy heroes, she updates her Web site, www.scribble-scribble.com.

Meet Me
IN
PARIS

SIMONA TAYLOR

KIMANI
ROMANCE

Once again, for Rawle and our two little funny-bunnies.
Thank you for the beautiful life we've built together.

KIMANI PRESS™

Recycling programs
for this product may
not exist in your area.

ISBN-13: 978-0-373-86129-3

MEET ME IN PARIS

Copyright © 2009 by Roslyn Carrington

www.kimanipress.com

Printed in U.S.A.

Hey folks,

Those of you who read my blog, The Scribble Pad, know I'm a scatterbrain. I'm always carrying on about something or other that I forgot to do or said when I shouldn't have. Well, what with my freelance work, my kids, my books, my blog, my passionate love affair with my kitchen, my reconciliation with my herb garden after a bitter breakup, my pets and the hunky love of my life, who wouldn't be a flake?

But you want to know how forgetful I was this time? I came *this* close to shipping off the manuscript for *Meet Me in Paris* without my "Dear Reader" letter. I must be nuts! This letter is one of the rewards for finishing the book. Why? Because I get to talk to you live and direct. One of the other rewards? When you talk back.

Over the past four years or so, I've worked at turning my Web site and blog (at www.scribble-scribble.com) into a fun community. You really ought to pass by and say hi.

I'm also reaching out to readers' groups from all over the world, just to find out what they've been reading and to let them know what I'm working on next. If you want to be on my mailing list, drop me a line. You can e-mail me (come on, tell me what you thought about *Meet Me in Paris!*) at roslyn@scribble-scribble.com.

You can also snail-mail the love to me at:

Roslyn Carrington
(or Simona Taylor, I can live with either one)
P.O. Bag #528
Maloney Post Office
Maloney
Trinidad and Tobago

and I'll bounce some right back.

Till then, take care.

Simona

Chapter 1

Gonna Be One of Those Days

First, there was the pantyhose. The last pair of pantyhose in the drawer, and silk ones at that. The last pair in the whole apartment, and considering the current state of Kendra's finances, the last one she'd be wearing until payday rolled around—and they had a run. Not a dinky, fix-it-with-a-dab-of-nail-polish sort of run, either. It was the kind of run that should be more truthfully described as a ladder, and a four-alarm fire engine ladder to boot.

Then there was the scorch mark on her silk blouse, a Japanese designer original, put there by Kendra herself when, in her irritation over the pantyhose, she'd accidentally set the iron to Wool rather than Silk. The mark snuggled in her left armpit, almost indiscernible, but it was a crime to ruin anything that gorgeous.

Naturally, when Kendra arrived at the towering Farrar-Chase building on Blackburn Boulevard, the elevator was down again. The cab sat forlornly in the lobby, its doors dismantled and its guts exposed, like the victim of a woeful accident. Workmen in blue coveralls stood around drinking coffee and solemnly contemplating the problem.

Kendra's workplace, the head office of the Wanderlust chain—renamed from Salomon's Travel and Tours a few months ago, when the new owner blew into town like a tornado—was on the sixteenth floor. Universe 3–Kendra nil. She sighed and began to climb the stairs.

By the time she reached her floor, it was nine-fourteen. Near the swinging glass doors, Mrs. Mertz was lurking, like a ferret who'd heard a rumor that there were nice fat mice on the loose. Lurking and smiling. No, not smiling, smirking. Her lipstick was a scary, bloodied scarlet, the same shade she had been wearing for years. Kendra was sure it was the only color she owned. "Nine-fifteen," Mrs. Mertz said. She tapped her watch, in case Kendra hadn't cottoned to the fact that she was talking about the time.

"Fourteen," Kendra corrected, and pointed to the wall clock. Childish, she knew, but the woman always made her feel like a kid.

"Whatever. You're still late." Her too-long eye teeth were tipped with red.

Kendra suppressed a shudder and hurried to her desk, ripping off her favorite Hermès scarf and, more reluctantly, her gorgeous Balenciaga coat, as it bared her laddered stocking for all to see.

Then Iris walked in, and Kendra felt a thumping at her temple, like the band striking up moments before the Titanic hit the iceberg. She hadn't even had her coffee yet. Iris's homing device led her unerringly toward Kendra's cluttered desk. "Busy?" she asked, and sat without waiting for an answer.

Kendra liked Iris well enough. The older woman was as

cheerful as they came, although her voice rose half an octave or so above the threshold of human tolerance. But, as many women did when they were flushed with the newfound joys of wifedom and motherhood, she waxed lyrical about the most unsettling things…and did so at great length.

"Uh…" Kendra hit the power button on her computer, knowing even as she did so that the old heap would take forever to get going. "A little," she hedged, all the while silently yelling, "Hurry, hurry! Boot up!"

Iris smelled of lavender bath salts and Cheez Whiz spread. She was wearing a necklace of spray-painted pasta elbows strung together with odd-shaped lumps of clay by her four-year-old. She wore it as reverently as if it were a string of pearls. On her right shoulder was the grubby handprint of her eighteen-month-old. It was Monday, and that inevitably meant Kendra would be treated to an expansive rundown of the weekend's antics by the tireless duo. She braced herself.

Iris leaned forward, eyes shining. "You won't believe this."

Try me, Kendra didn't say.

"Zachary did a huge poop last night."

Kendra nearly fell off her chair. "What?"

"He did a *huge* poop." She demonstrated with her hands—as if Kendra needed a visual. "And took his diaper off. All by himself. Then he showed it to us!"

Iris was smiling. Waiting for her to say something. Kendra coughed, searching for an appropriate response, but all she could come up with was, "Oh, really?"

"Right in the middle of Tony's cocktail party, would you believe it? Everyone was so impressed. He's so smart for his age. And then he marched inside, and brought out the tub of baby wipes."

Kendra fished frantically in her In-box. "Wonder if the mail guy passed," she said, a little louder than necessary. There was nothing there but today's paper. "Where is he?" All of a sudden

the impending appearance—or inexplicable nonappearance—
of the mail guy took on a disproportionate importance.

Iris amused herself during Kendra's mini panic attack by
fiddling with the array of knickknacks littering the desk, an as-
sortment of souvenirs from far-flung places in the world. They
were gifts from Kendra's grateful clients for trips she had
arranged. In the year or so since she moved here, she had become one of the best sales agents Salomon's Travel and Tours—
or, rather, Wanderlust—had. She loved people, and it gave her
the greatest pleasure to hand select the best holiday packages
around for the company's small list of wealthy and fussy
clients. They'd been assigned to her since her promotion from
sales representative to special accounts executive.

The computer finally obliged and chimed out its little welcome. Kendra tried not to look too relieved. This minor but sig-
nificant event had no effect whatsoever on Iris, who had moved
from a purple koala from New Zealand to a small Bahraini
hookah made of brass. Kendra tried again. "Busy around here,
huh?" That was when she noticed that, far from being simply
a broad hint, her comment was disconcertingly true.

She looked around. A soft buzz hovered above the heads of
the employees occupying the twenty or so cubicles on the floor.
Many were on their phones, and from the low, excited chatter,
she suspected they were talking to each other.

"You betcha, it's busy! Hammond's snarling mad. He's got
poor Petreena jumping through hoops. Making phone calls,
running around looking for documents…something's going
down. And from what I hear, it isn't pretty."

Kendra felt a chilly dread settle upon her shoulders. She
looked up. One of Shel Salomon's brilliant ideas had been to
erect the CEO's office on a huge loft overlooking the general
working area, and to construct it almost entirely of glass. That
way, he could—and frequently did—sit at his desk and look out
onto the floor, like a lion on a hillock surveying his pride.

The disadvantage, as Trey Hammond learned, was that, while the occupant watched his staff, they could—and frequently did—watch him. Because the new owner was a looker. With his long legs and lean, athletic build, he was the hottest stranger to ride into Santa Amata in ages. He had dark brown hair with a hint of warm highlights, skin the exact color of the filling in a Reese's Peanut Butter Cup, and charcoal gray eyes—gray eyes! And—the girls sighed—he had the most beautiful smile.

When he'd arrived, the whole office—practically the whole building—had gone into a frenzy of speculative whispers. Half the unmarried women, and a few of the married ones, related breathlessly to each other the details of their briefest encounters. In the elevator, in the lounge, at the cooler or the coffeemaker—everyone wanted to know who this newcomer was. And why hadn't he crashed into their lives earlier?

He was up in his glass box now, and Iris was right, he didn't look happy. Kendra watched with growing unease as he paced the carpeted floor, arms outstretched, gesticulating forcefully as he talked. Even from all the way down here, he was larger than life. The fine tailoring of his navy suit emphasized his height, and his obvious agitation made him seem to fill the large office. Hammond's executive assistant, Petreena Rai, swayed as she tried to continue facing her boss, even as he wore a path into the gold rug.

Kendra began to feel ill. "What d'you think he's mad about?"

Iris leaned forward. "Talk around the water cooler says he was in all weekend with the external auditors."

Auditors? Oh no.

"Talk says someone's been robbing the company blind!" Iris waited eagerly for Kendra's scandalized reaction, maybe for a little more information to feed back into the rumor mill.

Oh…God. I'm going to throw up.

Head hurting, mouth dry, Kendra stood and wheeled past

Iris, her only thought being to make it to the bathroom before she embarrassed herself.

Iris swiveled in her chair, concerned. "What's wrong?"

Bathroom, Kendra thought. Bathroom!

"Need some water? You aren't…" she looked around to see if anyone was listening, and then hissed in a voice that would unavoidably be heard by anyone who was, "You aren't pregnant, are you?"

Kendra managed to shake her head. Her phone started ringing.

"Want me to answer that? Want a paper bag for your head?"

Only if it comes with a cyanide pill, Kendra thought.

The phone stopped ringing. Kendra evaded Iris and hurried up the corridor. The ladies' room, and refuge, were in sight. Mrs. Mertz loomed, cutting off any hope of escape. "Miss Forrest! Didn't you hear your phone?"

"No, I…" Kendra answered weakly. "I…uh…was on my way to the ladies' room. I didn't—"

"I was calling you."

"I'm…sorry?"

"Mr. Hammond wants to see you in his office." This seemed to make her extremely happy.

Kendra hesitated, looking past the woman's angular shoulder to the swinging door with its familiar icon, a white-painted female in a triangular skirt. Had she been three seconds faster, she would have been on the other side of that door.

Mrs. Mertz followed Kendra's longing gaze to the bathroom door. "You're just going to have to hold it."

Just going to have to hold it? On any other day, she would have laughed off the directive, suggested to Mrs. Mertz that a cup of tea might improve her mood, and continued on her intended trajectory.

But not today.

Wordlessly, she turned, the terror that had replaced her initial dread eliminating any need to hit the bathroom anyway. She walked back into the main working area. Past her own desk. Mercifully, Iris had left. As she mounted the curved staircase leading to the CEO's office, she wondered briefly what Marie Antoinette must have felt like as she climbed the scaffold. At least the peasants weren't hurling insults and rotten cabbages in her general direction. Yet.

The big glass door was etched with the words, TREY HAMMOND, CHIEF EXECUTIVE OFFICER. Beyond it, she could see Hammond and Petreena. The latter was still agitatedly clutching her notepad, reading aloud from it. The former had stopped pacing, and was standing stock still. He was looking right at her.

In one imperious gesture, he motioned for her to enter. The soft pile of the carpet was familiar, as were the warm earth tones of the decor—harvest gold and pumpkin, olive green and cranberry. That was one thing Hammond hadn't gotten around to changing in the rampage of evaluation and modification he'd gone on.

The warmth of the office was in stark contrast to the demeanor of its occupant. Trey Hammond couldn't have been thirty-five, but his conservative suit made him seem older. His face was as somber as a graveyard. "Miss Forrest?" he confirmed.

"Yes." By rights, she should have extended her hand to shake his, but something told her he wouldn't be keen on taking it. She kept it at her side.

"Have a seat," he said. It was not a request.

In spite of her churning stomach, Kendra raised her head and held his stare. "I prefer to stand."

He lifted his shoulders and let them fall. "Suit yourself." The desk between them was littered with files, documents, and boxes of papers. Right before him, however, in a clear space among the rubble, was a manila folder.

He opened it and removed a single sheet of paper, glanced at it, and lifted his eyes to hers. The much-discussed gray eyes were now a flat, cold, gunmetal gray that sent chills down Kendra's back. Hammond held the document out to her.

When she didn't take it, he set it down, turning it around so she could read it. It was printed on the letterhead of a large and respected auditing firm, and appeared to be the cover sheet of the report that still lay in the folder. The word "fraud" leaped out at her.

When Hammond spoke again, she couldn't bear to look up. His voice was clipped, cold and disdainful. "Miss Forrest," he began, "can you give me one good reason I shouldn't call the police?"

Chapter 2

Busted

Deny, deny, deny. The liar's mantra. Even in the face of over-whelming evidence of your guilt, deny. But she was a lousy liar. Hell, she wasn't even a good thief. The piece of paper between them was a stark, accusing white. She looked away. As she did so, she caught sight of Petreena, standing anxiously nearby, head dipped, avoiding the unpleasant scene.

Kendra tried to catch her eye, pleading silently for the smallest gesture of support, but Petreena determinedly avoided her. If there was to be any tarring and feathering, she was loath to come anywhere near the brush.

Hammond caught the wordless exchange, and was merciful, at least toward Petreena. "Miss Rai, would you leave us?"

Petreena was off like a bullet, scurrying as fast as her pencil skirt—an excellent Givenchy knockoff that would have fooled anyone who didn't have Kendra's discerning eye—would let her.

Then Kendra and Hammond were alone. More damning papers appeared from some infernal place. Kendra recognized most of them.

"As you've probably heard, I've been meeting with managers, examining the books, and conducting a series of audits." He waved his hand. "Standard procedure after any takeover. Helps me understand where the company is and decide how I'm going to take it where I want. One of the auditors noticed something."

He stabbed at a piece of paper with a long finger. "Over the past few months, five payment vouchers were made up to cash, signed off and settled. All were charged to accounts you're responsible for, but my auditors inform me there's no way of determining whether the services being invoiced were rendered. Have they?"

Kendra said nothing.

"You should know, Miss Forrest. The signature on the vouchers is yours, I presume?" He waved one of the documents before her face. She flinched, but didn't need to look at it. Instead, she nodded.

"Have these services been rendered?" He didn't raise his voice, but the dangerous chill conveyed his anger. "Because if you're unable to verify otherwise, I'll have to assume the beneficiary of these payments—fourteen thousand, six hundred and eleven dollars in payments—is you."

Kendra expelled the breath she'd been holding. It hurt.

"So, let me ask you once again, is there any reason, any reason you can give me, why I shouldn't call the police?"

"Don't," she managed. "Please."

"Why not?"

She hated the way he was looking at her, taking in her short, glass-smooth pixie cut, carefully made-up face and hand-tailored business suit. The run in her pantyhose felt incongruous in comparison. His eyes moved to the emerald studs in her ears, and then to the matching tennis bracelet, pendant and ring. Her wristwatch wasn't one of a kind, but it was limited edition. She wondered if he could recognize Prada when he saw it.

From the contempt on his face, she was quite sure he could. "Why not?" he persisted. "An orange jumpsuit not your style? You got a problem with the county not providing emerald-studded handcuffs for its inmates?"

"That's unfair!"

"Unfair? Is fraud fair? And what about stealing money, falsifying invoices and milking your own employer, not once, not twice, but five times? How fair's that?"

"You don't understand!"

"What don't I understand?" He was asking a question, but he looked as though no answer she could give him would satisfy. "Did you or didn't you steal the money?"

"I'm not a thief!"

"Did you steal the money?" he roared.

"Yes!" she shouted back with equal amounts of chagrin and affront. Nobody raised their voice at her!

He gave her a cynical, satisfied smile. "Well, then, that makes you a thief."

Even in the face of her own guilt, she was mulish. "You can't talk to me that way."

"I can, and I am. And I have to say I'm disappointed. Your employee record is impeccable. Mrs. Mertz says you're a hard and productive worker…."

Kendra lifted her brows in surprise. Mrs. Mertz had said that?

"And it seems you've been promoted to special accounts executive faster than any employee in the history of the company. Even Shel Salomon seemed to like you. And you do something like this to him. He's going to be disappointed."

Kendra's heart sank. "You're going to tell him?"

"Why shouldn't I? In the few months we held negotiations, I've never known him to be anything other than a fair, decent human being."

"He's a wonderful person," she confirmed. "I've got nothing but respect—"

"You've got a fine way of showing it. He deserved more than to be gouged by a greedy, unscrupulous—" He halted his tirade with a sharp inhalation. Then he gathered up the documents— the evidence against her—and began replacing them in the folder. "So, what's it to be? Cops?"

"No!"

Hammond's eyes bored into her terrified ones. He seemed to be thinking. Kendra sensed she was balanced, barefoot, on the edge of a sharp sword. Which way would he make her fall?

"Very well," he said finally. He picked up the phone and dialed. "Mrs. Mertz, Miss Forrest is leaving us. Could you kindly supervise her as she cleans out her desk?"

"You're firing me?" she gasped.

He looked surprised that she had expected anything less. "Verbally, for the time being. You'll have formal, written notification from human resources delivered to your home by courier this afternoon. But right now I want you off the premises."

"But you can't. I need this job. I need the money!"

His gaze swept her clothes and jewelry again. "Obviously, you're a woman of expensive tastes. Nonetheless, I'm sure you'll agree I can't afford to keep an untrustworthy employee on staff."

She was outraged by the slur. "I am not—"

He cut her off with an upraised hand, as though he'd had his fill of the unpleasantness and wanted to bring an end to it. "If I were you, I'd consider myself lucky the company isn't pursuing prosecution." He gave her a hard, dismissive look. "If I were you, I'd leave quietly."

"But…." She flailed, unable to comprehend what was happening. Shock made her giddy.

"Good day, Miss Forrest." He sat heavily in his big chair, and folded his hands on his desk. His expression invited neither opposition nor further conversation.

Struggling to maintain her balance, Kendra turned and walked away. Mrs. Mertz was waiting outside the door. Kendra expected gloating, but saw instead a mixture of surprise, curiosity and the tiniest sprinkling of compassion. She accompanied her downstairs in silence.

From the moment she set foot on the floor, it was evident the glass office above had worked to her disadvantage. Although they could hear nothing that had taken place, everyone knew something was afoot. As she approached her desk in the wake of an electric silence, she could sense every pair of eyes upon her, even though all and sundry were steadfastly pretending to mind their own business.

From the rubble in the corner of her cubicle, she fished out a cardboard box and slowly began to fill it with personal items. Spare makeup kit, toothbrush and toothpaste, thesaurus and atlas, candy jar and bud vase.

She hesitated over the mess of knickknacks given to her by grateful clients. Tiny rum bottles from Barbados. A stuffed camel. A Brazilian rain stick. They were hers, weren't they? But if she took them, wouldn't they all be an indictment of her and the trust her clients had placed in her? Could she ever bear to see them again?

She packed in as many as could fit, and left the rest on her desk. It was enough to take a walk of shame in front of one's colleagues; it was too much to do it a second time just to pick up another box of stuff.

She said nothing as Mrs. Mertz, not being as mean as usual, silently took inventory of all she was taking, as per company procedure. Kendra signed her name at the bottom of the single sheet of yellow legal paper.

"Kendra," Mrs. Mertz began.

"What?" Kendra asked wearily. It was only a little past ten, and already she felt like she'd put in a brutal day's work.

"I know we haven't always…I know sometimes I can be a little…well…." She coughed self-consciously. "I don't know what made you do…this…."

Kendra looked away.

"But, well, it was a…a pleasure working with you."

If there was anything more that could have surprised Kendra today, that would be it. She'd always thought her supervisor had hated her guts. She'd thought she was a horrible, mean person. Maybe she'd been wrong about that, too.

"Thank you." There wasn't anything else she could say.

"Take care of yourself," Mrs. Mertz added. She sounded sincere.

Kendra nodded, balancing the box as best she could, and focusing dead ahead to blot out the gaping faces surrounding her, she walked out of the main doors and headed for the stairs.

Chapter 3

Devil Cuts a Deal

Kendra couldn't bear to unpack the box. She set it down on the floor inside her front door, and there it stayed. The lock on the door stayed closed, too. But she wasn't alone, fortunately— or unfortunately, depending on how you looked at it. She had the company of a few old friends she thought she'd ditched a long time ago: the seductive, unpredictable Miss Betty Crocker and those shameless old scallywags, Ben and Jerry.

For two days, she subsisted on turtle brownies topped with gobs of ice cream. The tight control she'd held for so long over her urges and her eating, was slipping. That scared her. But the feeding frenzy was welcome, too. It kept her mind off her the shame and guilt of what she'd done.

Every time she made it to her fridge door, Fat Kat was there waiting. The old photo was taped to the door, slightly askew.

More than once, caught in the act of helping herself to a spoonful of ice cream straight from the tub, or pouring shredded mozzarella into her mouth from the bag, she wanted to tear down the photograph, rip it into confetti, and toss it out the window.

"Don't condemn me," she told the photo. "You, of all people, should understand."

But the moon-faced girl with bad skin and a jumble of crooked teeth had a different expression each time. One minute she looked shocked, the other, disappointed. Pitying, condemning. Her old self, the teenage self she'd tried so desperately to leave behind, was in no mood to forgive.

Kendra couldn't blame her. What had she done? The escalating circumstances that had led to her scandalous downfall had begun with the best of intentions. First, tired of being overweight, fed up with feeling as if she always had to apologize for her size, she'd used every ounce of willpower to curb her eating sprees. Gradually, the weight had gone down.

Then there were her skin, teeth, hair—so many other things she still hated about herself. Getting that all fixed ate up a huge chunk of her savings. A dermatologist took up what was left. Then there were manicures, pedicures, skin treatments, pampering she'd never had in her life. And over the months, she'd started seeing someone in the mirror who didn't look half bad.

Then, none of her clothes fit. Although she'd always had a passion for fashion and a huge sense of style, she'd never liked herself enough to wear designer outfits before; but now, with a pretty face, pretty hair and pretty smile, she bought expensive clothes to show it all off. When she'd maxed out her credit cards, she applied for new ones. For a while she was as happy as a pig in mud. For the first time in her life, she'd stopped craving food. And the more she bought, the better she looked, the better she felt about herself.

Then the bills had started rolling in.

Kendra leaned against the wall and squeezed her eyes shut

at the memory. Fighting panic, going against all logic, she took cash on one credit card to pay off another…and kept on shopping. She'd replaced her old addiction with a new one.

The collapse came so fast, she'd barely had time to think. She missed a rent payment, an installment on her TV. She had a credit card cut up right in front of her—and then she missed another rent payment. It was awful. Crazy. And then, she'd been doing the finances for a project, her mind buzzing with the kind of low-grade panic that came with impending eviction, when she'd had an awful, desperate idea.

She filled out a voucher to cash.

She'd meant to pay the money back, had every intention of doing it. Then her car got repossessed. Her furniture was in the firing line. The credit card companies were calling, the bank was calling. So she filled out another voucher, and then another one….

"I'd be ashamed of me, too," she said softly to the accusing photograph of the old her. With nausea bubbling insider her, Kendra dumped her last pint of ice cream into the sink and threw the last two brownies into the trash. "I am. I just wish…" Wished she could do something. Take it all back. Make amends for what she'd done.

Fix it.

Her mind spun around to the office…and Trey Hammond. His disgusted stare, his complete rejection of her. She wasn't what he thought she was, she wanted him to know. Not really. She was a good person.

A good person who'd done a bad thing. What could she do to get him to believe her?

All that night, she sat in an armchair, too wired, too exhausted, too filled with remorse to sleep. She watched the sun come up, pale and watery, and watched the numbers on the clock tick away until she was sure Wanderlust was open for business.

Then the phone was in her trembling hand.

"Wanderlust, good morning. Trey Hammond's office. How may I assist you?"

"Petreena?"

"Kendra? What're you doing calling here?"

"I need to talk to Mr. Hammond."

The hesitation lasted maybe a second and a half, but to Kendra it was vast. "I don't know if that would be the best thing."

"Petreena, please."

"Kendra, you shouldn't be calling. I don't think he'd want to talk to you."

"Just ask him. I only need a few minutes."

"Well, he's, uh, in a meeting."

"What meeting?"

"That's confidential." Click.

Somewhere in the back of Kendra's skull, steel doors slammed shut. Leaving her out in the cold like a ragged beggar. No, she wasn't giving up like that. She hit redial.

"Wanderlust, good morning. Trey Hammond's—"

"Petreena."

Petreena's tone was a combination of embarrassment, anxiety and irritation. "Kendra, I don't think—"

"Petreena, please. Help me. We used to be friends."

"I'm not too sure about that…."

To be spit out so easily, like a pebble in a spoonful of rice. It shouldn't have hurt, but it did. For a dizzying moment, she had the sensation of blinking out of existence and then flickering back. If you were denied by people who knew you, did you cease to exist? She accepted her demotion from friend status with grace, but insisted, "Well, we were colleagues, at least. You've had coffee at my desk. We've split lunch. For the sake of that, if nothing else, please let me speak to him."

The hesitation was longer this time. Then she heard a series of clicks and blips.

"Miss Forrest."

The hand holding the receiver had gone cold. It took great effort not to let the phone fall to the floor. "Mr. Hammond, I need to see you."

"What about? I thought we'd already said all that needed to be said."

"Please, I need you to know I'm sorry."

"I'm sure."

"I mean that. You have to believe me. I made a mistake and I'm sorry."

Hammond's deep voice was deceptively melodious, but what he was saying was poison. "Miss Forrest, time is money, and you've taken up enough of both of mine already. If you want to apologize, fine. That's neither here nor there with me. But if your conscience is pricking you, I suggest you find a priest. Absolution is their job, not mine. Now, unless you have a check for fourteen thousand dollars that you'd like to drop by with—"

"I've got nowhere near that—"

"Then we have nothing more to say to each other." The next thing she heard was the dial tone. She stared at the receiver, looking for answers. After a few minutes the phone kicked up a howling that wasn't half bad, given that it penetrated the silence in the apartment, at least for a while. Instead of clicking it off, she set it down on its side, and let the jarring, obnoxious noise spur her into action.

She took a shower, allowing the hot water to soak away the despair and self-disgust of the past few days, and then surveyed the contents of her closet. Hammond had made a nasty remark about her expensive taste in clothes. That meant he could recognize a genuine designer original, as opposed to a knockoff. As much as she adored the sheer beauty of a well-designed outfit, the last thing she needed was to wear something that would set him off again. Chloe would just have to chill out on the rack for a while. She chose a simple navy shirt dress with long sleeves and a modest hemline. With the kind of eating frenzy that had overcome her over the last few days, she half expected to have ballooned beyond all logic; but it fit her 132-pound frame as perfectly as it had the day she'd bought it. She brushed her short cap of hair, smoothing it down carefully and wrangling it into its pixie shape with holding gel.

Makeup? A little mascara, maybe, and a warm shade of lipstick. Enough to look dressed rather than provocative. Not enough to look vain or self-absorbed. Her pumps were all business and no flash, but she drew the line at giving up her hand-tooled Spanish leather handbag. After all, a girl has to have something to bolster her confidence when she went to seek out a very mean and dangerous fire-breathing dragon.

Kendra stood staring up at the sixteenth floor of the Farrar-Chase building. It was lunchtime, and Blackburn Boulevard was humming like a beehive. The bank of four glass revolving doors at the top of a short flight of stairs were practically whirling as workers spilled out of the building and down onto the sidewalk. Even on this overcast, slightly windy spring day, they were cheerful, chatting in their pairs and threesomes.

The determination that had fueled her thus far abandoned her at the foot of the stairs. Could she really do it? Could she walk past all those desks and cubicles, feel the burning stares at her back, hear the hushed conversations, and know they were about her? And that glass office, Shel's eye in the sky. Speaking to Hammond in there again would leave her naked. Stripped.

The doors spun again—and out walked chatterbox Iris. Fluffy as a lemon meringue, chubby legs having difficulty with the stairs. Smiling and laughing with Jennifer from procurement.

Panic! Kendra darted back to the curb, squeezing herself between a hotdog cart and the newsstand where she always bought her papers. The newsstand owner gave her a funny look, but didn't comment.

If she couldn't go in there, she'd have to come up with an alternative battle plan.

An ambush was her next best bet; the man had got to come out sometime. Bachelor style, he never brown-bagged his lunch and never ate in his office. He prowled the restaurants within a block or two of here, a habit everyone in Wanderlust had grown accustomed to. She could only hope he kept up his pattern today.

But, as had been the trend these days, she was long on hope but short on luck. She watched other employees leave and return, watched Iris and Jennifer saunter back in, and still no sign of Hammond. Round about one thirty, it began to rain. And why not?

She was glad for her camel coat, and even more glad the newsstand owner didn't seem to mind her huddling under his narrow eave for what little shelter it afforded her. Was the man ever going to come out to eat?

Then, in one of those uncanny moments where everything seemed to have been choreographed by someone with a flair for the dramatic and a deeply ingrained sense of irony, the door on the far right spun again. Out strode Trey Hammond, larger than life and twice as striking. He descended the stairs like a huge ticked-off puma. Long legs eating up the sidewalk, mackintosh open down the front, coattails unfurling in the slight breeze, as though he didn't care if he got wet. He was limber, graceful, and filled with purpose. Unbelievable, Kendra thought, he even walked like he was on slowed-down film. The only thing missing from the scene was Miriam Makeba on the sound track, warbling the refrain from "The Lion Sleeps Tonight."

His brows were drawn in an expression that was either pensive or irritated. Her money was on the latter.

Just before he passed the newsstand, she blocked his path. "Mr. Hammond." Her voice hadn't betrayed her. Good.

The irritation was replaced by surprise. It took several seconds for him to get over the shock and speak. "You're aware, of course, that stalking is a crime."

Ha ha. Funny. She clarified for his benefit. "I'm not stalking you. I was waiting for you."

"But I've told you I don't want to speak to you. Since I don't desire your company, doesn't your persistence constitute stalking?"

She was tired, hadn't slept for three nights, and her glycemic load was through the roof. She tried to be calm and explain her position as best she could. "Look, Mr. Hammond, all I want is two minutes of your time."

"Why?"

He really did make her feel like she was in the presence of a huge feline. Even standing still, he was thrumming with pent-up energy. His solid, powerful body dwarfed hers, and his eyes held her in thrall. Cats were known to mesmerize their prey with a stare, weren't they? She almost forgot what she was about to say.

"I want you to know how sorry I am." Ah, yes, that was it.

"You've already said as much."

"And you need to know I'm not a bad person. I'm not a thief."

Unblinking, he still had her pinned. "Miss Forrest, I think we've gone over this ground already, and frankly, I'm a little tired of it. I didn't brand you a thief. You did yourself that disservice."

That was when the wall of fatigue caved in. It was the wrong time, and definitely the wrong place, but walls had a habit of doing that. And on the way down, it crushed every shred of self-esteem she had left. Horror of horrors, her eyes were burning and her cheeks were wet, and the moisture was a whole lot warmer than the rain. She put her hand up to hide the evidence of her weakness, but it was too late.

Hammond knew tears from rain, and wasn't impressed. "Oh, please. Spare me the theatrics."

"What?"

"I know exactly how women like you operate. What you can't achieve by stealth you achieve by guile. Did you think that leaving your couture outfits and five-hundred-dollar shoes home would impress me with your humility? Did you think that turning on the waterworks would soften me up? For what? What d'you want from me?"

She held her hands out, empty, pleading. "Your understanding."

"Not interested."

"Your forgiveness, then."

"Not my department. Refer to my previous statement about visiting a priest." He fished in his pocket, and she had the ludicrous feeling he was going to subject her to the humiliation of offering her a few coins, bus fare, maybe, and suggesting she get the heck out of his face. But he withdrew a folded, pale blue kerchief and handed it to her. She stared at it in wonderment. Were there really still men who carried those around?

"Mop yourself up," he advised her. "You're making a scene in front of my business."

The gall of him! "You don't own the whole of Farrar-Chase, you know. It was here long before you rode in on your hoss and tried to take over. It'll be here long after you're gone on your way. There're at least twenty travel, decorating, new media and marketing businesses in there."

"Yes, and one of them is mine. You can keep the hankie." He spun around and walked off.

She did as she was told, scrubbing at her face to remove the tears and the streaks of makeup they'd left, catching the newsstand owner out of the corner of her eye and wondering how much of their conversation he'd heard. The fine linen, rubbed hard into her skin, abraded away her despair, her humiliation and her pain. Then there was only one emotion left. Pure, home-grown, unadulterated, polyunsaturated rage. It was all she needed.

Hammond was walking so fast she could barely keep up, but sheer pig-headedness made sure she did. Two blocks down, he turned into the Blarney Stone, a pseudo-Irish steakhouse she'd been to once or twice. She followed at a distance. He never so much as looked back.

She made it inside a minute and a half after he did. It was good to be out of the drizzle. She could see Hammond seating himself. A waitress was upon him in a single shake of a lamb's tail. He ordered with a smile that was happily returned by the young lady, who was leaning in toward him a little more closely than necessary. As she walked away, the waitress flipped her hair and gave her shamrock-dotted hips a little swivel. Ick.

Look at him. Sitting there so smug and self-satisfied. Flirting with the waitress. Loading up on breadsticks, as if everything was all hunky-dory, now that he'd given the least likely candidate for Employee of the Month the slip. The more she thought about it, the more she paced. Getting madder and madder.

On her dozenth about-face on the lobby carpet, she found herself toe-to-toe with the hostess, who was all kitted up as a leprechaun. Central casting would have been impressed. The young woman was four feet ten and festooned with stick pins, smiley-face stickers, shamrock key chains, small, fuzzy animals and clunky brass whatnots. She looked like a walking trinket cart at the county fair. "Miss? Will you be dining?"

The apparition jolted Kendra out of her internal rant. She was suddenly aware she must look quite bizarre, half-soaked, whirling back and forth in the lobby, muttering as though she had imaginary friends. She felt her face heat up. "Um, not right now." She tried to sound nonchalant.

"Are you waiting for someone?"

"You could say that." Involuntarily, she glanced across at Hammond. He was poring over the menu. Still completely relaxed, damn his eyes.

"Then would you like to have a drink at the bar while you wait?"

A drink? In here? She probably didn't have enough change

in her purse to buy herself a soda. She shook her head. The leprechaun gave her a strange look and left.

Missy with the swively hips brought Hammond a Bloody
Mary. Again, the goo-goo smile as she set it down, and again
his overwhelming charm as he took it. All this with the ease
of a man who'd rid himself of a minor irritant, like he'd
brushed a beetle off his coat sleeve. Like she, Kendra, was
nothing. No.

Next thing she knew, she was standing at his table. The expression on his face was so precious, if she could have bottled
it, she'd have made a million bucks. She took advantage of his
momentary speechlessness to lay into him. "Listen up, Hammond. I've had enough of you and your attitude. What makes
you think you can sit in judgment of me? Where d'you get off
acting so superior?"

"Where do *you* get off hovering over my table while I'm
having a drink? For God's sake, Forrest, if you're going to ruin
my lunch, at least do it sitting down. You're making me dizzy."

"I don't want to sit down. I want you to listen. I've listened
to every nasty thing you've had to say to me—"

"Was any of it undeserved?"

"Be quiet. It's my turn to speak. I've changed my mind. I
don't need your forgiveness, because you're a rude, arrogant,
self-assured bastard, so coming from you, it wouldn't be worth
a damn. But I do expect you to respect me. Don't you ever, ever
turn and walk away from me again. Don't you ever call me a
thief again. I did something stupid, and I admit it. And I don't
have the money right now, but I'll get it to you if I have to work
my fingers to the bone…." She waited for the sneer. She waited
for the derisive laughter. None came.

"Okay."

Okay? That was it? It took the wind out of her sails. What
next? They stared each other down like two cats balanced on
an alley wall. His stare was thoughtful, contemplative, making

her feel like a beetle under a magnifying glass. She hoped he wasn't directing the sun's rays at her.

She couldn't stop him from looking at her, but while he was doing it, darned if she wasn't going to take the opportunity to size him up, too. He must have known how good looking he was. Why else would he have chosen a suit that was the exact charcoal gray as his eyes? Why else would he have worn a shirt the color of a glacier's heart, and a tie of garnet that set those coals alight? His silver-rimmed glasses framed his face so well, he could have stepped down from a poster in an optometrist's window. No wonder he knew the brands she was wearing. He was a bit of a metrosexual himself. And they said *women* were vain.

His almond-hued skin was clear and bright. His soft, slightly wavy hair was closely cut and razor-marked. Even so, it rippled from forehead to nape. His finely shaped nose was indisputable evidence of mixed blood. His lips…she didn't want to go there. As she watched him, and as he watched her, something in his face changed. She could have sworn that the deadly steel of his eyes warmed to a deeper shade. Maybe it was that shirt again. He gestured at the chair opposite him, the one she was clutching. "Sit down. Please."

She sat, discovering that she was heaving with effort.

"Feel better?"

"What?"

"That was a whole lot better than the crying jag back there, wasn't it?" Unbelievably, he was smiling. Kindly.

She did a quick mental inventory and discovered that she did feel better, but she wasn't going to admit it. Not to him. So she didn't say anything.

He didn't seem perturbed. "What're you drinking?" he asked, lifting his Bloody Mary as a visual example. She realized she was dying of thirst. Again, there was the problem of her empty pocketbook. That, and the laughable idea of drinking with the enemy. "Nothing."

"Oh, come on. Storming all the way over here and reeling off a list of my character flaws to the entire restaurant must have made you thirsty. What's your poison?" He signaled the waitress without waiting for an answer.

"Water, please."

"I'm buying." He didn't say it in a nasty way.

Perceptive. But she insisted. "I like water just fine."

He sighed. "Have it your way. Still or sparkling?"

"Tap."

Looking amused by her stubbornness, he turned to Miss Shamrock and said, "The lady will have a glass of water. Tap."

Witnessing Kendra's tirade hadn't diminished the redhead's effusiveness toward Hammond, but it did earn her a scathing look, of which she got a double helping when the woman returned with a tall, frosty glass of water. She accepted it gratefully and took a long, deep drink.

He handed over the glossy, emerald-green menu. "The mutton here is amazing."

Was he for real? He couldn't be inviting her to have lunch. He didn't even like her, never mind respect her. Was this masochism or just another way to make her squirm? "I'm fine, thank you." But the smell of the hot food all around tugged at her will, hooking her by the nose like a finger-shaped wraith straight out of Saturday-morning cartoons. Food, her personal demon, always beckoned when she was nervous or upset. Right now, she was both.

"Dieting?"

"No." Her two-day binge aside, there was no way she'd ever put herself into the position where she'd have to do that again. Not after she'd done so much hard work. She shook her head to underscore her denial.

He accepted it without question, and offered, almost irrelevantly, "My wife used to diet all the time." That was when she noticed the simple, ridged gold band on his wedding finger. He was married? Someone put up with *him* 24/7? She hadn't heard anything about *that* in all the breathless conversations about him and his indisputable gorgeousness back at the office. She was *sure* her colleagues would have noticed a ring. Maybe she was just odd woman out. Or hard of hearing.

He cajoled. "Come on, you've got to be hungry. It's way past lunchtime."

Food. Food! She shook her head, not trusting herself to speak.

Patiently, he explained, "Hey, I'm starving, but my mother didn't raise me to eat in front of a lady, if she isn't having anything. So please, it's almost two o' clock, and I haven't had breakfast. Pick something, or I'll do it for you."

All she could do was sit in dumb incredulity.

He took that as a cue to proceed, and summoned the redhead again. "We'll both be having the mutton."

She spent the rest of the meal struggling with the disorienting sensation that she was having lunch with Trey Hammond's good twin, or at least the pod person that had replaced him somewhere between the steps of Farrar-Chase and the front door of the Blarney Stone. Her lunch companion was urbane, almost friendly, making small talk about the travel business and asking her opinion about a deal he was exploring. She answered where applicable, hearing her own voice as though it were coming from underwater, but couldn't scrape up the gumption to initiate a train of conversation herself. The food was delicious, a comforting place to hide. She drew the line at his offer of desert, so they sipped Irish coffee to round off the meal.

He steered the conversation around to her personal life with the suddenness of a rally driver at the Paris-Brest-Paris. "Are you from around here?"

"Where?" she asked stupidly, irrationally looking about the room.

He laughed. The sound was foreign to her ears. "I wasn't enquiring as to whether you were born under the salad bar. I meant, are you originally from Santa Amata?"

"No, not exactly. I've only been here for a couple years or so. I'm originally from Gary."

"Indiana?"

"Yeah." She paused to allow him to insert the obligatory Michael Jackson reference, but was disappointed.

"And what brought you out east?"

What, indeed. Getting into too many details about her past would have meant digging up the flat-footed, ugly duckling self she'd tried to escape, and Kendra was never keen on that. She was deliberately vague. "I guess I needed a fresh start." And she'd made one, a good one, until she'd gone and messed it up.

"So you went to college, stayed in Indiana for a few years, then moved here. And you worked with Shel ever since?"

"Yes. He hired me because of my travel-and-tourism and hospitality courses. This was my first real full-time job. Not much tourism in Gary. I felt like I found my niche here."

"Wet behind the ears, huh?" The irony couldn't possibly be lost on him, but he chose not to rub it in. Instead, he finished his coffee and set the spoon in the saucer, next to the cup. He folded his hands on the table, and tilted his head to one side, examining her contemplatively. Calculatingly. Slowly.

Lord, she wondered, what next?

Finally he spoke. "Did you mean what you said?"

"What part?"

"The part about working your fingers to the bone to pay me back."

"I did. I'm going to pay you back, no matter how long it takes. I don't know how I'll get a job in the travel business, considering how small the community is. They must all be talking about me. And it's not like…." She looked at him, then glanced away. "It's not like I'm leaving Wanderlust with a glowing recommendation." In spite of the grimness of the situation, she laughed ruefully. "So I guess I need a whole new career."

"People have short memories. It'll blow over faster than you think."

Easy for him to say. "It might, or it might not. But I will pay you back. I promise."

Tired from the events of the day, he took a deep breath, as if he were drawing on inner courage to say what he had to say next. "You could pay it off in kind."

"What?" For a second, she wondered if she could get away with throwing her glass in his face. He'd been forbearing so far about siccing the police on her. Would such a gesture of feminine outrage end with her in the slammer?

The shock on her face brought a short, amused laugh to his lips. "Don't jump to conclusions. That wasn't what I meant, but I'm flattered you think I'm capable of such a sophomoric idea. I was more in the market for a housekeeper."

A housekeeper? "You've got to be kidding me."

"No, I'm not. I've been living out of a hotel for the past few months, and I've only just settled on a house. I've had my stuff delivered but it's still all in boxes, and the place's gonna need a little elbow grease…."

"You want me to unpack your stuff and clean your house?"

"Pretty much. It'd go a whole lot faster if two people tackle the job."

"Two people? What about your wife? Isn't she helping?"

"My wife is dead." Briefly, the chill in his eyes was back, but it was gone so fast, she could have imagined it.

Oops. I'll have a side of fries with that mouthful of my own foot, please. "I'm sorry."

He nodded. "Thank you."

She contemplated his incredible offer. Was he tripping, or was she? On what planet could such a proposition possibly make sense?

He leaned forward, looking at her levelly, challenging. "Too demeaning for you? Afraid to get scuff marks on your Manolos?"

He couldn't resist that, could he? "You leave my wardrobe out of this."

He lifted his shoulders. "I was just thinking we could help each other out. You need money, and I need help. I certainly don't condone what you did, but I'm in need. I'd pay eighteen dollars an hour, that's above standard rates around here, I'm told. You could get half in cash, and the other half I put toward your debt to me." He added, "When you get another job, you can feel free to take it up. Then we can make alternative arrangements for repayment. That is, if you really are serious about paying me back."

She lobbed his challenge right back into his court. "Aren't you afraid I'd swipe your spare change off your nightstand?"

"I doubt even you would stoop that low."

Even her? Oh, he was a bastard. But she couldn't see any other way out of her predicament, and he knew it. He knew it so well, he wasn't even making any further case for himself. He just sat there, quiet, allowing her to wrestle with her own misgivings and come to the realization that he had her over a barrel.

Times might be tough, but she still had her dignity. She'd show him. She wasn't afraid of a little work, and she certainly wasn't as self-absorbed and high-maintenance as he thought she was. Plus, who knew how long it would take her to find another job. So, he wanted to make her pay for her sins in sweat? Bring it on.

"When do I start?"

He pulled out a thin, stylish pen from his breast pocket, scribbled an address and number on a paper napkin, and pushed it to her. "We'll start on Saturday. I'll be home all day, so I can show you around. Eight o' clock. Don't be late."

As if.

Chapter 4

Atonement

If Kendra was going to change her mind, she had a day in which to do it. Truth be told, she came pretty close. Half a dozen times she made it to the phone. Half a dozen times she reminded herself that, if this was a battle of wills, Trey Hammond wasn't going to win. If it was a test of her character, he wasn't going to find her wanting.

She was so determined not to be late on Saturday, she slept with one eye on the alarm clock, checking it periodically to reassure herself it was set for the right time. She was up with the chickens. She showered and dressed in sturdy jeans and a plain, long-sleeved, brushed-cotton shirt, throwing on a pair of rugged boots to show Hammond she meant business. She bolstered herself with a bagel and some cranberry juice and marched out of the house well on schedule.

The crumpled napkin bearing Trey's address was a wadded ball in the front pocket of her jeans, but she'd read and reread it so many times she knew it by heart. His new house was in Augustine, a nice professional area favored by many of the black, Hispanic and Asian businesspeople in Santa Amata.

By bus, it was a convoluted trip. The ones that did the city circuit didn't cross Falcon River. She had to go all the way down to the main bus station and change there, and even so, it was still a twelve-minute walk from the nearest bus stop. She stepped up her pace a little. It wouldn't do to lose her time advantage as she was closing in on the finish line. Would he be beastly enough to dock her wages?

Wages. Of all the harebrained schemes. Here she was, a young, bright professional, about to ransom her soul back for the queenly sum of eighteen bucks an hour. She checked her watch. Four minutes to eight. She resisted the urge to run. The man wasn't going to get her goat.

There was a storybook quality to his street. It was nicely laid out, with orderly rows of pastel-colored houses and duplexes. Yards were separated by neat hedges and filled with tree houses and kennels. Some of the swings and slides were occupied, even at this early hour. Children laughed and screamed, chasing excited dogs and each other. Then she was standing in front of Hammond's house, double-checking the number on her beat-up paper napkin, although she knew she had the right place.

Surprise left her rooted to the sidewalk. This was the house he'd bought? A mild breeze could have knocked her over. She'd have bet good money Hammond would have chosen an environment as cold and stark as he was. She was expecting chrome, white paint trimmed with gray or black, and a precision-cut lawn. Instead, she got a new millennium version of Norman Rockwell. The air was filled with a hint of fresh paint. The two-story house was a blushing ivory, with doors, windows and gables trimmed in a pale, milky squash. The slanted shingle roof was a deep avocado, and the window panes stained in gemstone colors. Spring was springing up all over. In contrast to the other yards in the street, the grass was a knee-high tangle dotted with stray daisies. A seesaw and jungle gym stood in the far corner, all lonely.

Yellow-bellied sapsuckers and copper-crested whatchama-callems flitted deliriously around, feasting on bugs—and on bananas that somebody had stuck on the branches of the fruit trees that were just pushing out new blossoms. Hammond, a nature lover? Nawww.

Out of the corner of her eye, she saw something move in one of the curtainless ground-floor windows. Remembering her purpose for being here, she stopped gawking at the lawn and straightened her shoulders.

The front door swung open. "You going to stand there all morning, or are you coming in?"

Deciding the question didn't warrant a response, she opened the waist-high wooden gate that led up the flagstone path and met him on his doorstep. "Good morning," she said as amiably as possible. "Lovely day. How you doing?" *Let's see him try to grouch his way out of that one.*

"Morning," he answered, pleasant as pie. "And I'm fine and dandy, thank you." He was actually smiling, and glory be, his face didn't crack. "What about you?"

"Oh, I'm…" It was about then she noticed he had on the best damn fitting jeans outside the pages of a magazine, and a stark white, sleeveless undershirt that he'd probably just pulled from the package. She could still see the creases in it. His feet were bare. What a difference clothes made in a man! What had happened to the young Turk with his custom suit, striding around the office as if all of Wall Street depended on his performance? The man who stood before her was relaxed and comfortable in his glowing skin. His skin, while she was on the subject, made her think of hot toast done just right, dripping with melted butter and deep, rich honey. Oh. Food.

His lean, fit body spoke not of hours of pumping iron but of good health, natural grace and the kind of structure that only came from good genes. The dark brown hair that sprinkled his chest and peeked out from his armpits as he held the door open was slightly curlier than the crisp, well-tended mass upon his head. Kendra, Kendra, stop staring. Even though he was as dressed down as she, she felt almost grubby by comparison. She patted down the front of her shirt in a nervous gesture she hoped he didn't spot. Fat chance. Those gray eyes didn't miss a thing. "You look ready to get your hands dirty."

"I am."

"Good. Had trouble finding the place?" He almost gave her the impression he was interested in the answer.

She shook her head. "No, but it was a pretty long ride."

He checked the time. "Still, you hit eight on the nose. What'd you do, sit up all night in a chair fully dressed, just to be sure you'd be on time?"

"Of course not," she replied with a huge helping of scorn. Not exactly. She stepped in so he could close the door.

He slipped into tour guide mode. "The house is about fifteen years old, but in good repair. I've had some work done, but more to suit my taste and my needs than to fix any problems." He led her into the living room, gesturing as he went. There were traces of workmen's mess, bits of wood and rubble in the corners—and guess who was going to have to clean it. "I've knocked out a wall here to make things more airy, see?" There was a hint of pride in his voice, a homeowner's excitement at the freshness and promise around him.

She didn't begrudge him his satisfaction. He'd made this castle his own, and was proud of it. "I see. It's very nice."

"My den's back there." He pointed. "Bedrooms are upstairs, one master, one guest, and one's for a…" He trailed off, and then started over. "One's a child's bedroom. I haven't figured out what I'm going to do with that one yet."

"I saw a seesaw and some other kid's stuff in the backyard. I guess a kid used to live here, huh?"

"I guess."

She should have known better, by the look on his face and his noncommittal answer, but before she could stop it, she was cheerily saying, "It'd be a lovely house for children. Lots of space, places to play. Did you ever want children?"

He looked as though she'd whacked him in the gut with a four iron. He took an age to answer, and when he did, his eyes were steady on her face, as if he was afraid to blink. "My wife and I never had the chance."

Oh God. The late wife. She hastened to apologize for her clumsiness. "Oh, I'm so…"

He shook his head, and the uncomfortable moment was past. "Forget it." He started moving again. Motion. Good. He continued with his tour, as though she'd created no ripples on the surface of his pond. "Kitchen, of course." He gestured through the open back door. "There's a deck out there. The wood needs stripping, but I'll have to get to that later, when the interior's in order." He laughed lightly. "If I ever make any friends here in Santa Amata, maybe I'll hold a barbecue. I've been here only a few weeks and it's been all work."

Kendra peeped out politely, but her mind was still on her faux pas. "It's…lovely."

His spiel returned to the kitchen. "They delivered the appliances yesterday, but the gas isn't hooked up yet. We'll be ordering take-out for lunch. Gas people are supposed to swing by this afternoon, so maybe soon you can taste my hand, as my grandma used to say. Fridge works, though." He opened it, partly to demonstrate, partly to offer her something. "Had breakfast?"

Last thing she needed right now was to see food. Being on

the brink of a self-imposed sentence of community service was nerve wracking enough. "I'm okay."

"Doesn't exactly answer the question, but all right. How 'bout some juice?"

"Thank you."

He reached into a cardboard box, rummaged through packing peanuts and retrieved a glass, which he washed and filled with pink grapefruit juice. "Ice maker needs about twenty-four hours to kick in," he apologized, "but the juice is sorta cold."

She sipped it. "It's fine." They were standing next to the marble-topped island in the kitchen, with him a little closer than she would have liked, given that she'd suddenly discovered that he had quite a body on him, and that as much as she didn't cotton to him, her body wasn't immune to the ripples she could see as he folded his arms across his chest. He looked at her, assessing, until she couldn't stand it anymore. "What?"

"I half wondered if you were going to show."

Smart aleck. "I said I would, and I'm here." She couldn't resist adding, "Just because I've got sticky fingers doesn't mean that my word isn't my bond."

He nodded to indicate that her barb had landed well, but didn't volley back.

She tried not to sound too disgruntled when she added, "You have to admit you have me over a barrel, Mr. Hammond. I don't have many options open to me right now."

"Trey."

She frowned, puzzled, so he clarified. "Call me Trey. Please."

In a bug's eye. "At the office we called you Mr. Hammond."

"We're not at the office. In my home people call me Trey."

She wasn't in the mood for an argument, so she said, "Okay," but she wasn't going to call him a damn thing, if she could get away with it.

"Can I call you Kendra?"

"You've called me worse."

He stepped maybe two inches closer, but two inches was enough for her to catch the slightest whiff of his scent. Sawdust and aftershave. And something else, something manly and warm, but she had to be imagining that. "If we're going to work together, can we at least make peace?"

The swirly patterns the grapefruit pulp made on the sides of her glass suddenly held her attention to such an extent that she was unable to meet his gaze. Peace. He didn't know what he was asking. He'd questioned her morals and mocked her values. He'd thrown her out in front of people who'd once respected her. He'd reduced her from a woman in a prestigious position to a scullery maid. Now he wanted peace.

He was waiting for an answer, but not in silence. "I'm not the enemy, Kendra. We're just two people helping each other."

She wasn't so sure about that. "I don't…"

"Try, at least," his voice was low, encouraging.

She caved in like a house of straw. "Okay." The concession took less effort than she'd expected.

"Okay." His smile lit up his eyes. He held out his hand.

She took it, idly noticing how, although she didn't have the most delicate hands in the world, his was still capable of engulfing it. She noticed, too, that his skin was as warm as his voice. This was probably the first time she'd touched him, and, considering what that brief contact was doing to her, she was going to do her darnedest to make sure it didn't become a habit. She pulled her hand away and rubbed it surreptitiously on her jeans. "We should get started." It was hard to get the suggestion past the little frog in her throat.

He conceded without any argument, easing the glass from her fingers and putting it next to the sink. "We'll start with my den." She followed close behind, and came to stand near a pile of cardboard boxes in a corner. He was a careful mover. On the sides of each box he'd clearly written the word "Den" with a fat, black marker. She didn't need much of an imagination to visualize other piles of boxes elsewhere labeled "kitchen, bathroom, bedroom." Just one more way in which this man kept his world under strict control. Just one more way in which they were different.

"I thought we'd fix this one up first," he was telling her, "because I like to have a nice quiet place to work in at night."

Odd reason, Kendra thought. When you live alone, isn't the whole house a nice quiet place? Setting up a den in order to have a "quiet place to work" was like building an igloo on a tundra just to have a place to cool down. He was oblivious to the irony. She didn't draw his attention to it.

"Back in a sec." He disappeared, then returned with an armload of cleaning supplies—buckets, mops, brooms, cleaning fluids of all kinds—and set them down. She reached for a broom, but he beat her to it, and began to tackle the rubble left behind by the painters and repairmen. He caught her look of surprise. "Did you think I was planning on sitting back with a bourbon and watching you work?"

That was exactly what she was thinking, but she'd rather drink cleaning fluid than admit it. "No, not exactly," she fluffed.

He stopped sweeping long enough to tell her, "I'm not a slave driver, Kendra. I expect you to put in a fair day's work, and I'll do the same."

"I guess that's reasonable." Her surprise was being replaced by admiration for his decent gesture, but she wasn't about to let him see that, either. "I'll go fill this bucket, so when you're done sweeping I can mop up."

"Attagirl."

By the time she was back, he'd produced a small CD player and was loading it with albums. "Music to work by. Hope you aren't one of those modern girls who won't listen to anything that's not on the charts this very second, 'cause I'm old-school." He certainly was. The player began belting out vintage funk, loudly and with great enthusiasm. James Brown. The Average

White Band. Rick James. Chaka Khan. And he was right—it was music to work by. Before long, she forgot why she was here and focused on what needed to be done. She forgot that he was, if not the enemy, at least only a guarded ally. Together they found their rhythm.

When the floors were clean, the rug rolled down and the desk in place, they started to unpack his books. The walls of the den were lined on three sides with built-in, floor-to-ceiling shelving. When she first noticed them, she'd thought they were a little excessive; but now that his collection was being revealed, crate by crate and box by box, she was half-worried there wouldn't be enough room.

She took her time unpacking, reading the covers curiously, trying to gauge the nature of this surprisingly complex man. He was sentimental: he'd kept books from his boyhood, reading primers and adventure stories. *Hardy Boys* and *Treasure Island.* He was an escapist. There were science fiction, murder mysteries and legal dramas—John Grisham, Peter Benchley, Stephen King and Walter Mosley. Even more surprising, he had a collection of books on maritime nonfiction. Wars, war machines, boats and planes. These made her brows shoot up.

He caught her look and shrugged. "We've all got our vices."

Amen to that, she thought. At least his weren't fattening. As she helped him mount a framed MBA from Howard next to a twenty-year-old certificate of excellence in piano, Kendra had the odd sense that the wall of cold air she knew him to be was condensing and warming up into a human being. It was as if he was a huge puzzle that needed solving, and the items in all these boxes were the pieces.

She opened a box of knickknacks and photos. The one on top was fairly faded. It showed a tall, well built, sandy-haired, golden man with slate-colored eyes. He was standing behind a small boy on a bright red bike, his hands steadying the handlebars. Kendra recognized the frown of concentration on the boy's pointed face. She held the photo up. "You and your dad?"

He knew which photo she was referring to without having to look up. "Yeah. I was five. It was my first bike. I got it for my birthday. Well, Christmas and my birthday, I guess. They're both on the same day."

"You're a Christmas baby?"

"Unfortunately. You know we get about forty percent fewer presents over the course of a lifetime than regular folk?"

She made a rueful face. "Sorry to hear that."

He gave an exaggerated shrug. "You get used to it."

She looked down at the photo again. "Your dad's white?"

He shook his head. "Not exactly, but he could pass, if he'd had a mind to. If my mother had a mind to let him."

"Which she didn't."

"Nope."

She set the photo carefully down in the area of the bookcase they'd set aside for display items. "Are your parents…"

"Alive and kicking. Both retired, still living in the house I grew up in, a few miles outside of Atlanta. Been there ever since, until now."

"You're a southern boy."

"Yes, ma'am."

"Thought I heard something in your voice."

"Can't shake it. Wouldn't want to."

She rummaged in the crate and withdrew a larger, professionally framed photo. He was all grown up, embracing a beautiful, long-limbed woman on a boat. One arm was around her waist, the other cradled her cheek as she leaned against him. The woman had striking, exotic features, perfect Brazil nut skin and cheekbones sharp enough to draw blood. Her mouth was like a firm fruit, and her makeup looked as if it had been airbrushed on by a fine artist. She bore herself with the poise and elegance of royalty. Kendra felt the slightest chill ripple through her. Trey's wife, no doubt. She peered closer. Trey was relaxed, happy, smiling, gray eyes full of warmth, humor and life. His lips were parted, teeth white, Adam's apple faintly visible past the button-down shirt he wore. She almost couldn't recognize him as the same man.

"My wife died six years ago. Her name was Ashia. She was from Somalia." Somehow, he'd managed to stand behind her without her realizing he'd moved. Watching her watch the picture. In her embarrassment, she almost dropped it. "I didn't mean…"

He didn't answer. Instead, he took the photo from her fingers and placed it tenderly on his desk. When she glanced up several moments later, he was still looking at it. She couldn't read his face. She went back to work, feeling as though she intruded. Trey left the photo alone and joined her.

The next few boxes were full of model airplanes and ships. "Wonders never cease," she murmured.

He laughed. "A passion I haven't shaken from boyhood. I used to love making model planes and aircraft. These were modeled after authentic wartime craft."

"You made these? From scratch? No kits?"

"Some of the older ones are from kits. Look, this is a German Dornier Do-17. See the fat snub nose? They called it the Flying Pencil. I made it when I was thirteen or so. It's one of my personal favorites." He took up a tiny one emblazoned with a rising sun. "This one's Japanese. A Mitsubishi A5-M. Very fast. I made hundreds of kit models before I got bored. Drove my mother crazy."

"I'll bet." She was warmed by the pride in his voice, and enchanted by the glimpse he was allowing her into the boy he had been.

"My room was so full of models I could barely move about. We used to have ring-down battles twice a year or so. She used to make me throw half of them out. Wasn't prepared to live in a junkyard, she said."

"Pity. If you'd saved them you could have made a fortune selling them alone."

"I'd sooner sell my own soul," he countered. "You can imagine what it was like when I started making my own out of whatever bits and pieces I could drag home. My mother's junkyard metaphor took on a whole 'nother dimension."

She found herself chuckling with him. When the box they were working on was empty, she lifted the lid off another, and unpacked a heavy, wrapped object. Peeling away the layers of bubble wrap, she discovered a ship in a bottle. A rather *old* ship in a bottle. The shape, the feel of it, transported her back in time. She held it up to the sunlight. The ship inside was exquisite, its sails fully raised, even slightly curved, as though billowing in a gentle breeze. She didn't know the first thing about models, but she could see it was handcrafted. "This one's a beauty. It looks old. Where'd you get it?"

He was on her like a pouncing cat, snatching it from her hands. "Don't touch that." She watched openmouthed as he picked up a new piece of cheesecloth and rubbed it down, as though her fingerprints would contaminate it. There was a wooden stand in the box where she'd found the ship. He pulled that out, dusted it off just as carefully and placed the ship upon it on the main shelf, at the center of his collection.

She didn't know what to say. Didn't know how to react, feeling awkward and ashamed, but still unable to determine the exact nature of her crime. "I'm sorry. I…"

He wouldn't even look at her. "Maybe we should break for lunch." Not waiting for her response, he threw the cheesecloth aside and walked off. She followed, not bothering to hide her confusion. What had she done? What had she said?

As the wadding on the kitchen chairs hadn't been removed yet, they ate Chinese take-out, cross-legged on the floor. Throughout the meal, and after, Trey tried to act as if nothing had happened, but the camaraderie of the morning was broken.

She was glad when the afternoon was over. At five o' clock he called it a day, and walked her to the door.

He handed her a plain white envelope, and she knew without having to open it what it held: half her day's wages. She took it, face and neck hot with embarrassment over all it implied. She shoved it into her jeans pocket, out of sight.

"Thank you," he told her. "You were a big help."

She nodded wordlessly. They stood there on the doorstep facing each other, Trey appearing even taller because he was one step above. It was as awkward as that charged moment at the end of a blind date when both parties wait for someone to say or do something to break the tension…except she wasn't waiting on a kiss, she was waiting on an explanation—or an apology. She didn't get one.

Instead, he asked, "Tomorrow? I know it's Sunday, but I'll be home all day, and I was thinking we could get the living room straightened out."

Like I have a choice, she thought. But there was a pleading in his eyes that gave her the odd feeling he didn't just want her for her work. He wanted her for her company. Damn. Handsome, smart, self-assured, top of his game Trey Hammond is lonely. Don't that beat all. She nodded. "Tomorrow."

Chapter 5

Cruel Words and Accidental Kisses

The next day, Kendra was dead on time, even without getting paranoid over the alarm clock. The reduced Sunday traffic made the commute a breeze. She even had time to enjoy the short walk into his street and listening to the sound of children laughing in the gardens around her. They made her think of the forlorn seesaw in Trey's backyard, and his pained response to her innocent question. Something told her he'd picked this neighborhood for a reason, consciously or subconsciously. Whether he knew it or not, Trey Hammond was nesting.

She walked boldly up his stone path, and again he met her at the door. "Morning. Come on in." He was doing his darnedest not to let on how happy he was to see her, but the curve at the corners of his lips gave him away.

"Can't sneak up on you, huh?"

"You might be able to, once I get my curtains. It's good to see you. I—"

"Thought I wouldn't show?" she challenged.

"I knew you would. You promised. I was about to say I was waiting on you to get the waffles going. Batter's done, just sitting there. I thought you'd like them hot."

"Waffles?"

"It's Sunday. Technically, you shouldn't be working at all. I thought a hearty breakfast would start us off right."

"Oh." That sounded good—and intimate.

He noticed she was holding something in her hands. "What's that?"

She held up the small paper bag. "Nothing special. There's a fruit stand a little way up the road. I got two overripe mangoes for your birds. I thought they might…" She trailed off. It seemed like a good idea at the time, but now it felt idiotic.

"Oh, man, that's wonderful." He opened the bag and peered inside. "They'll love these. Thank you." He headed for the front garden. She noticed that—bless him—he was wearing the same pair of jeans as yesterday, and though slightly more grubby than they had been, they had the same fabulous fit. He'd used another clean white tank top from his stash. He really needed to buy his clothes in a larger size.

She stayed where she was, glad his back was turned so he wouldn't see how much she was enjoying the sight of him walking barefoot in the grass, stretching his arm upward to spike the mangoes on the jagged branches, where only the limp, dried-out peels of yesterday's bananas were left. As he walked, butterflies and bugs rose from the grass and swirled around him like leaves caught up in a dust devil. He dusted off his hands with purpose as he returned to her. "Good. We've fed God's little creatures, now let's see what we can do about ourselves."

Sounded good to her.

He walked her into the kitchen. Among all the mess and

clutter of yesterday, there was a clean spot on the table. Upon that, he'd laid out cream, honey and fruit preserves.

"Been to the supermarket, I see."

"The guys hooked up my gas yesterday evening, and then it hit me that the stove wouldn't do much good if I didn't have anything to cook on it. So I went on a shopping spree." He threw open the doors of his stainless steel fridge and gestured inside like a male version of Vanna White. It was loaded to the gills.

"You going to eat all that before it spoils?"

"I'm sure as hell gonna try. So…" He washed his hands at the sink and dried them on a dish towel. "You eat waffles, right?"

"Who doesn't?"

"Nobody in their right mind."

She watched him work. There was a cast-iron waffle iron on the stove. She could tell by its rich, dark patina that it had seen some use. "Your mother's?"

He pretended to be offended. "Oh, please, girl. Just because a man knows his way about the kitchen doesn't mean he's swiped half his mother's stuff. I've had this iron since college. There's a griddle and a skillet to go with it, too."

She was hesitant to risk further offending him by asking whether he'd made the batter from scratch, but then she spotted the mess of flour and sugar on the counter and had her answer. There was a sizzle as the batter hit the waffle iron, and like Pavlov's dog, Kendra licked her lips. This man was always offering her food. Her one weakness. How'd he know? She patted her hips and murmured, "Looks awful fattening."

He took his attention away from his cooking to look her over as slowly as he had in the restaurant. "Fishing for compliments?"

"I was certainly not fishing," she huffed. He must think she was *so* vain. His crack about emerald-studded handcuffs came back to her, and she wondered, was this how it was going to be today?

"I didn't mean that like it sounded. I was trying to pay you a compliment, but it came out wrong. You look great. You really don't need to worry about your weight."

If he only knew.

"Sit down. These'll be ready in a sec. Pour yourself a cup."

She sat obediently, lulled by the scent of berries, the warmth of the kitchen and his quiet efficiency. He served her first, urging her to eat up while her waffles were still hot, and in minutes his were done. He made congenial conversation, plying her with melted butter and honey, seeming anxious to make up for his rebuff of yesterday. Again, she sensed that loneliness rather than hunger was his motive for trying to prolong the meal. When they were done, she set down her cutlery with a satisfied sigh. She was proud of herself; she'd been relaxed enough not to feel the desire to go overboard with her eating. "Congratulate the chef for me."

"I'll pass it on as soon as I see him." He lifted a newspaper off of a small stack. "Sunday paper?"

She had to put her foot down. "I'm here to work, Trey. Remember?" It was the first time she used his name out loud. How easily it came to her!

Trey replaced the paper, abashed. "Right. Sorry." He pushed his glasses up on his nose with a purposeful, let's-get-down-to-business gesture.

"'S okay."

They rose together. "I cleaned up all the rubble and junk in the living room, so we can get straight to work." He was already ahead of the game. The furniture was all laid out. Again, she noted his excellent taste in fine things. The sofa and armchairs were made of good leather and wood, with elegant, well-crafted side pieces. He'd gone as far as to hang a painting on a wall. It was African. Somali, she guessed.

"Did you work through the night, or what?" she joked.

"Pretty much," was his sober answer. "A body's need for sleep is grossly exaggerated."

"Yeah," she agreed doubtfully. She began stripping off the plastic in which the furniture had been wrapped. He joined her, making short work of the heavy binding tape with a pair of shears. Again, their work took on a certain rhythm; but last evening's uneasiness hung in the air. By midmorning the furniture was clean and carefully rubbed down with walnut oil, and the elderly cushion covers had been replaced. A forty-two-inch plasma screen dominated the wall, and Trey was taking small speakers out of their packing case and setting them up in that mysterious configuration only men understood.

There was still a case of books to unpack—glossy coffee-table books meant to be put on display rather than read. As she gathered a few in her arms, one slipped from the top of the pile. She bent forward to pick it up. Bad timing. Trey was crossing with a large cardboard box in his arms, and didn't see her. He went down like the Colossus of Rhodes—right on top of her. She yelped, more out of surprise than pain.

"You okay?" He put his arms around her and lifted her off the floor, as if he didn't know or care how much she weighed. Large hands were running up and down her arms, checking for damage. Around them, a blizzard of packing peanuts fell. He was *touching* her. He'd already knocked half the wind out of her with his unscheduled landing, and surprise had robbed her of the rest. Now he was picking peanuts out of her hair and patting her down with a look of concern on his face. Hands passing along her skin. And he expected her to be able to draw enough breath to say something?

"Kendra?" His hands were on her upper arms, their tour of her body over, now that he'd assured himself there was nothing broken.

"I'm…I'm fine. Don't worry about…" Then, inexplicably, she was laughing.

He gave her a bemused smile, as if trying to figure out

whether he should join in her laughter or check her head for bumps. "I give up. What's so funny?"

"I don't know. Your face, I guess."

"What about my face?"

"You looked like you were about to lay an egg."

The image made him grin, but he said sternly, "Why not? This is serious. I don't weigh fifty pounds, you know. I could have hurt you."

"You didn't. Relax. Let's get back to work."

"No, you relax. Sit down. I'll get you a glass of water."

"No, Trey, I'm…" But she was talking to an empty room.

He was back with a glass. She didn't need it, but to make him feel better she drank a few sips, emptied the rest in a potted plant when he wasn't looking and set to work. The interlude had done its magic; the mood was light once again. Now that his sound system was set up, he didn't need his dinky little CD player. Today he was feeling more mellow, playing The Roots, Lauryn Hill and Wyclef. At one point, Kendra glanced up and noticed that they were bobbing their heads in concert to the beat. He noticed at the same time, and they both laughed.

Eventually, he got up. "What say we take a break?"

She had no problem with that suggestion. Her legs were going to sleep. She stood up and did an awkward dance to shake the blood back into them.

He delved into his massive fridge and returned with two beers. Thirsty now, Kendra took a long, unladylike swig. She leaned against the fireplace, gazing up at his Somali painting. Like everything else in his house, it was beautiful, done in tones of ocher and sienna.

"Kendra…" She jumped, spinning around. He was standing right next to her and she hadn't even sensed his approach. What was it with this man? Was he part vampire?

"Yes?"

"I have to say something. I feel awful about the way I acted yesterday. About the ship in the bottle. You didn't do anything to deserve that."

"No, I didn't."

"I'm sorry. I was rude and I apologize. It's just that…" He sighed and hesitated. "That was the last present my wife ever got me. It was a Christmas present. It means a lot to me, and I'm…a little touchy about it."

She should have guessed. "I'm sorry. I didn't know."

"You couldn't have." Behind the glasses, his eyes were the color of clouds weighed down with rain. She read his six-year-old pain and was amazed at how fresh and raw it still was.

"I'm sorry," she said again, but this time it was for his wife.

He misunderstood. "Forget about it." But he didn't move away.

Compassion flooded her soul like liquid light. The only thing she wanted to do right now was make him feel better. But how?

He looked down at his hands and realized he was still holding his beer. The expression on his face said: *How did this get here?* He set it down on the mantel behind her. As he leaned forward, his face brushed past hers. Panic. Bright and sharp. She knew what he was going to do a millisecond before he did. All he had to do was turn his face, just an inch or two, and his mouth would be on hers. He did, and it was.

But before she could decide whether to respond or not, or rather, before she could obey her body's command to respond, it was over. Trey sprang away from her like a cat on fire. He passed his hand over his head, rubbing it like it was sore. She watched, puzzled, as he paced. "That didn't happen," he muttered.

It certainly had, and she had an all-over body tingle to prove it.

He was back like a yoyo, standing before her. Frowning. "I didn't mean to—"

"Forget about it," she lobbed his own instruction back at him. Why was he so upset about something she'd actually…*enjoyed?* If anybody had a right to be upset, it was she. The past day and a half had taught her he was a little more human and a lot more tolerable than she'd thought, but that didn't mean she actually *liked* the man. Not enough to be thrilled he'd lost his head and kissed her. So why was *he* freaking out? "It's not the start of Armageddon," she pointed out.

"You don't understand."

"Seems I don't understand the first thing about you."

He made another fumble at apologizing. "I'm usually better at controlling myself. I don't know why I…especially with someone like…"

Oh no, he didn't say that. "Someone like me?"

"That didn't come out right."

"How did you mean for it to come out?" she demanded. She was still holding her beer, and found herself confronted with a choice: whack him with it, or set it down and storm away. She chose the option least likely to have her wind up behind bars. Her bag was in the kitchen, right where she left it. She shouldered it, doubled back and headed for the front door.

He tried to cut her off in the tiny vestibule. "Kendra—"

She didn't want to hear a word of it. She got her own two cents in before he could even get started. "Listen, Trey, I was willing to give this a go. Contrary to what you may think, I'm not afraid of putting in a little elbow grease. And I was grateful for the chance to make amends. But you know what? I'm not going to stand around and let you insult me. Especially not after you—" *Kissed me so sweetly.* As she drew back the heavy deadbolt, he wedged himself in between her and the door. He was a six-foot wall that she was either going to have to climb over or blast her way through. Which was fine with her. She shoved him, but he didn't even lose his footing.

"Don't go. Please. I'm an ass. That's probably the dumbest, cruelest thing I've ever said to anyone."

"If it wasn't, I wouldn't like to know what was." She pushed

on him again, her mind racing around for another escape strategy.
Kick him in the shins? Bite? "Out of my way, you big—"

"Forgive me. Please." He trapped her arms in his big hands,
trying to restrain her. "I don't know what's wrong with me.
Seems every time I turn around, I say something stupid. Every
time I speak to you, I owe you an apology. What I said was
reprehensible—"

"Tell me about it."

"But please don't go. Don't do this to me."

Physically overpowered, she chose the high ground. "Trey
Hammond, you are restraining me against my will. Let me go
right this second or I'm going to call the—"

"Kendra…"

"I'm going to scream!" She threw back her head, opened her
mouth and took a deep breath. No sound came out. No sound
came out because he'd covered her mouth with his again. She
couldn't tell whether the gesture was prompted by a desire to
silence her, or simply by desire, but he was kissing her and
kissing her good. If she was going to say anything else, it had
completely left her mind. This kiss was nothing like the last one;
that had been impulsive, almost accidental. Light and sweet.
This one overwhelmed her with its intensity. His mouth was
hard and demanding, crushing hers. She should have protested,
struggled to free herself from the hands that held her pinned.

But a crazy heat rushed through her like dried-up chaparral
on fire, wooshing down upon her and forestalling any notion
of resistance. When he released one of her hands, instead of
smacking him across the face like an outraged damsel was
supposed to, she curled it around his neck, pulling him closer.
He took his mouth away long enough to move to her throat, and
the brush of his lips there set off a seismic jolt that she could
feel all the way down to her toes. Her mouth was free, so she
could breathe again. She gulped in air, but it wasn't enough.
She was vaguely aware of her bag hitting the floor.

That white undershirt that moved with him, clung to him, was getting in her way. She pulled at it, yanking it up out of his jeans so she could feel the bare skin of his belly. The hair under her fingers crinkled. But that wasn't enough; she wanted to feel more of him, see more of him. With the near-psychic perception that arced between two people with a single purpose, he understood this, and peeled off the shirt. It fell on the floor next to her bag. He knew, too, that she was beyond the point of making a run for it, so he released her other hand, leaving them both free to roam his back and chest. He was all muscle, a contoured sculpture covered in lambskin. As she let her hands skate down his back and around to the front, across his navel, he shivered violently, groaning.

"Nobody has…" He stopped and tried again. "Nobody's touched me like that for…" He squeezed his eyes shut as though he couldn't bear to let her peer into him. "Oh God." He pulled at the front of her shirt, clumsy, unable to figure out the buttons. She opened them for him. Hooray for front bra clasps; he figured that one out all on his own. Each breast was a handful. Often, she was embarrassed by their size. Not now.

As he stroked her, he called her name again, softly. "Kendra…"

"Trey?"

"Touch me again."

She placed the flat of her hand against his belly, relishing the ripple the light contact caused. "No, here." He took her hand in his and moved it a few inches higher, until it rested over his heart. His heartbeat was a staccato thump in her palm.

He was hard against her belly, so real, so tangible, that she had visions of his nakedness. He released one breast again, almost reluctantly, to run his fingers though her short hair, and then leaned forward and did something so unexpected, so outrageously erotic that she let out a scream. He flicked out his tongue and let it run from her temple, past her hairline and into her hair, like a mother cat grooming her kitten, once, then again.

The vestibule wasn't big enough for them anymore. It no longer suited their needs; it was too narrow and too…vertical. Kendra had a better suggestion. "Trey?"

His voice was a rasp. "Yes?"

"We could…why don't we…"

Then a creak, the groan of unoiled hinges, and the front door swung open. They turned in unison, to see a woman standing there, hands over her mouth, staring at them in shock.

"Mom!" Trey gasped, and his glasses clattered ignominiously to the floor.

Chapter 6

The Lying Game

Like a pair of mongooses transfixed by a cobra, Trey and Kendra froze. Then he sprang away from Kendra, looking as confused and embarrassed as she. She felt his hands at her breasts and realized to her horror that he was hastening to do up her bra. She brushed his hands away and did it herself, wrapping her shirt front across her like a cloak. *God of thunder, lightning and rain,* she prayed fervently, *strike me down. Now.*

Trey turned to face his mother. "Mom! What're you doing here?" He glanced behind her into the yard, but there was nobody there. "Where's Pops?"

The poor flustered woman flapped her hands like the wings of a flightless bird. "My goodness gracious! Oh, Trey, baby, I'm so sorry!" She reached out and took Kendra's hand. "Oh, girl, forgive me for being such a clumsy old woman. If I could bury my head right now, I swear…"

"It's okay," Kendra lied. But her mortification wasn't enough to stop her from searching the woman before her for signs of her son. She was about Kendra's height, and maybe fifteen pounds heavier. Her ruthlessly dyed black hair was rolled up in a twist. He certainly hadn't inherited her eyes; those, she knew, he'd gotten from his father. But the long face was all his, as was the fullness of the lips. She was darker than him, but that stood to reason, too.

Trey picked up his glasses, examined them, and finding them unbroken, put them on. The brief distraction allowed him to calm down enough to ask again, "Where's Pops, Mom?"

His mother pursed her lips and lifted her head, turning toward her son with that look all mothers got when they weren't prepared to be argued with. "Your father's at home, where he always is. In front of the TV, watching the game."

"What game?"

She waved her hands dismissively. "How should I know? Whatever's on. You'd probably know that more than me, being a man and all. Now go get my bags."

At the same time, Kendra and Trey noticed two large suitcases and a carry-on bag on the doorstep, all brand-new, in a riotous paisley design. "Your bags?" Trey echoed inanely.

She pointed them out with her thumb. "Bags. Those." When he didn't move for three seconds, she added, "You still standing there, boy?"

Trey stepped to it. As the woman sailed past Kendra, she stopped to pat her sympathetically on the cheek. "You okay, sweetie?" Kendra managed a mute nod. The woman went inside, leaving them alone again.

Kendra took in Trey's stunned face. She couldn't decide what was more mortifying—that she'd been caught half naked by Trey's mother, or that she'd been, at that moment, inviting him upstairs to his room to take things further. Was she out of her ever-loving mind? She stepped aside to let him pass with the bags. What should she do next? One thing was for sure: she was

not going back in there. She'd been leaving, hadn't she? She
picked up her bag from the floor where she'd dropped it, tossing
in odd bits and pieces that had rolled out: gum, lipstick, keys.

He knew what she was thinking. "Please," he begged. "Don't."

Surely, he was kidding. Before things had gotten out of hand,
she'd been mad at him. She'd been storming out, before he kissed
her so soundly she didn't know which *way* was out. But her departure had only been interrupted, not forestalled. Later, gator.

They could see his mother poking about in the living room,
and Kendra didn't need to know the woman to know she
probably had sharp ears. Trey kept his voice low. "Don't go yet.
Please. Let me get to the bottom of this."

"But I—"

"Just a few minutes. That's all I ask." He looked so miserable
she didn't have any choice other than to relent. Knowing she
was making a big mistake, she followed him.

Trey's mother was approvingly feeling the texture of the
new cushion covers. "Nice. I like it. You two will be happy here.
I can tell."

You two?

Kendra tried to catch his eye, but he studiously avoided her.
Instead, he set the bags down next to the sofa and said "Mom,
you haven't answered my question."

His mother looked guilty, but headstrong in the face of it.
"What question, son?"

"What're you doing here? And where's my father?"

"I answered the second half."

"Well, answer the first half."

"You haven't even kissed me. What's that about?"

Trey softened. "Sorry, Mom. I just didn't expect to see you
here." He kissed her on both cheeks, and they hugged. "Why
didn't you call me? Why didn't you tell me you were coming?"

She smiled sweetly. "I know how persuasive you are. You'd
have talked me out of it."

"I'd never have done that. I'm thrilled to see you."

"I wasn't afraid you'd have talked me out of coming to see you, sweet pea. I was afraid you'd have talked me out of leaving your dad."

Trey gaped. "Leaving him? What d'you mean?"

"Exactly what it sounds like."

He looked dazed. "Why?"

"'Cause he's boring."

"You walk out on a man after forty years of marriage because he's boring?"

"Women have done it for less."

Trey slapped his forehead in frustration. "Mom, listen, you've been through a lot. It's been a hard year for you. Aren't you being a little hasty?"

She snorted. "Like I have all the time in the world to think about it. And speaking of time, don't worry, I'm not moving in with you. I'm here for two weeks or so, then I'm heading down to Key West to meet your aunt Amelia. We're going on a trip. To Egypt. Always wanted to see the pyramids. And camels. Never seen a camel."

Trey looked like a vein was going to burst in his head. "Egypt? That's suicide!"

"Why? I've got my meds. And I'm sure there are some very good hospitals in Egypt, if worse comes to worst."

"You won't have the chance to find out what the hospitals are like, because you aren't going. I forbid it."

Her black eyes narrowed and hands went to her hips. A whole foot shorter than he was, Trey's mother looked like a feisty hamster getting all up in a cat's face. "You *forbid* it? Oh, child, you watch who you're talking to. You might be big in your britches now, but I'm still your mother. I haven't given you a mouthful of soap in more'n twenty years, but let me tell you, I'm not all that opposed to the idea."

The thought of his mother trying to make him eat soap was so wacky that he broke out in a grin, but a glare from her cut him dead. "Sorry, Mom," he apologized humbly. "I'm worried about you, that's all."

"Well, you can stop worrying. I know what I'm doing."

"Mom, I own a travel agency. At least you could have come to me to—"

"Oh, shush." Trey's mother concluded her examination of the furniture and went on to the books, picking them up and holding them close to her face. Either she'd forgotten her reading glasses, Kendra concluded, or she was too vain to wear them. She noticed Kendra hovering, trying to be invisible. "Oh, you poor thing! I'm so rude. Leaving you standing there like the cheese. Especially after practically catching you in flagrante...."

Trey rolled his eyes. "Mom, we were not *in flagrante*. We—"

"Oh, please. I may be old, but I'm not blind." She stepped forward to Kendra and offered her hand. "I'm Marlene Hammond. You must be Natalie."

Kendra had barely enough time to pick her jaw up off the floor. "Me? Oh, I'm—"

Trey stepped in before she could say any more. "Sorry. My fault. It's me that's being rude. Sweetheart, this is my mother...."

"Call me Marlene," his mother interjected. She was grinning like the Cheshire Cat, leaving Kendra wondering what streak of madness ran in this family.

"And this is Natalie."

She shot him a look that was a combination of disbelief, shock and anger. Who was Natalie? And why was he—

"Oh, baby, it's so nice to finally meet you." Marlene flung her arms about Kendra and kissed her on both cheeks. She stepped away, holding both her hands and gave her the once-over. "You didn't tell me she was so lovely, Trey."

"She is, isn't she," he said softly. Over his mother's head, his eyes were pleading.

Kendra was almost robbed of speech, but managed to say, "Thank you, ma'am."

"Marlene."

"Marlene."

His mother leaned forward to whisper loudly, "I can't tell you how happy you've made me, child. I'd all but given up on Trey ever finding anyone. Poor boy, so bogged down in his miseries. But he's come halfway across the country, and here you are. God bless you."

What did you say when someone invoked blessings on you? If you didn't deserve them, did they turn into curses? "Thank you."

"Thank *you,* sugar. I just know you'll be good for him. I mean, love is love, and Lord knows, my son loved Ashia. But six years is six years, and—"

Trey wasn't going to take any more of that. "Mom, come into the kitchen. You shouldn't be standing around in your condition."

Marlene allowed herself to be guided to the kitchen, but laughed. "You and your father. Always doing your best to make sure I do nothing. Can't fathom it. There'll be lots of time to do nothing when I'm dead." Kendra's face betrayed her shock. Marlene clarified cheerily, "I'm dying. Didn't my son tell you?"

Kendra threw him a murderous glare but tried to act neutral for Marlene. "Uh, no, he didn't. I mean, he's talked about you…" At least that was true. "But he hasn't said anything about…that."

Marlene patted her left breast. "Two heart attacks in one year. Not a whole lot of time left on the meter."

Kendra was horrified. "Oh my goodness, are you in any pain?"

"What, with the drugs they give me? I see more pink elephants than you can shake a stick at. Trust me, when you get to this age, the diversion's almost worth it—ooh, nice fridge." Marlene yanked open the double doors and launched an investigation. "Trey, you going to offer your mama something to eat? Airline food, ha. In my day, they used to feed us like princes. Crab. Lobster, too. Then some young smarty-pants decides to cut costs. Next thing you know, we're all eating apples out of paper bags. Like horses." After twiddling around with whatever caught her eye, reading labels and shaking bottles, she withdrew her head, smiling. "I see you're taking good care of my son, Natalie. He's got enough food in here for a party."

Kendra didn't know what to say. The look she lobbed at Trey said, *your ball*.

"I shop for myself, Mom."

"Then how come I don't see any frozen pizza or microwave mac 'n cheese?" She sniffed a cantaloupe. "Yum." She waved at the kitchen table. "Y'all sit yourselves down. I haven't cooked my son a meal since he left Atlanta."

Trey tried to intervene, although he should have known better. "I'll fix you something. You've just been travelling for hours…."

Marlene's scowl could have wilted lettuce. "Sit down."

"Yes, ma'am." He sighed and sat next to Kendra.

For Kendra it was lunch in the Twilight Zone: Trey being attentive to her. Marlene chirping away, calling her Natalie and avoiding any mention of Trey's father. All Kendra could do to vent her frustration was shoot him a dagger every time Marlene's head was turned. He absorbed them meekly. When their meal of canned soup, grilled cheese subs and fresh cantaloupe was over, Trey took control. "Mom, now I have to insist. You need to lie down for a little."

"But I'm not even tired. I want to see the backyard…."

"You'll see it later. Right now, you're going to take a nap whether you like it or not."

Kendra could see the lilac shadows under Marlene's eyes, and was glad when the token protest was over and she gave in. Trey took his mother's arm, easing her gently up out of her chair and toward the stairs. "My room's the only one fixed up right now, so you'll take that one. I'll sleep on the couch until I can set up the bed in the guest room."

Marlene protested. "I can't throw this poor girl out of her room!"

"Natalie has her own place on the other side of town, Mom."

"Where?"

He floundered. "She's in…"

Aha, Kendra thought. That's one thing you never bothered to find out about me while you were having me investigated. She could have left him swinging, but for Marlene's sake said, "I live in Catarina. It's a little neighborhood on the other side of town."

He telegraphed his gratitude. She didn't send a receipt.

"Well, I hope you move in soon. Save on costs. Two can live as cheaply as one, you know."

The absurdity of living in such close proximity to this disturbing man made Kendra flush hot all over. Marlene spotted it and said gleefully, "Ah-ha! There you go. She's wondering why you haven't asked her yet. The girl's sweet on you and you're dragging your feet. What's wrong with you, boy?"

Let's see him get out of that one. Kendra waited, brows arched, smiling her challenge.

"I'll…try to rectify that." Trey tried to coax his mother into refocusing on her purpose. "Come, Mom, let me help you up the stairs."

Marlene wrenched away. "I'm perfectly capable of navigating a flight of stairs on my own, young man."

He grinned. "I'm not that young."

"I'm not that old." Marlene flounced upstairs. Trey brought up the rear with her bags.

Kendra stewed in her own juices while waiting for Trey to reemerge. What was going on? Who was Natalie? And why was she being dragged into this?

In the time he took to come back down, a new Ice Age could have fallen. "Sorry. I had to make sure she was settled and took her meds."

Uh-huh. And he wasn't stalling for time up there. Well, too bad. He was back downstairs now, and that meant he was all hers. She pounced. "Trey, what's this about? Who's Natalie, and why does your mother think I'm her? Why didn't you say different?"

He regarded her soberly, and found he didn't have the words. He walked past her, back into the kitchen, and opened up a cupboard.

Kendra was hot on his tail. "Don't you walk away from me. I demand an expla—"

"I don't think beer will cut it right now," he muttered. He withdrew an unopened bottle of aged Scotch and poured out generous portions. "Ice?"

"No."

He handed hers over. It burned on the way down. He came near, and leaned against the kitchen wall.

She waited on hot pins and needles while he finished his drink. "Come on, spit it out. Who the hell's Natalie?"

"Natalie's nobody."

Typical male, dismissing some poor girl like that! Could he be more callous? "I may be a lot of things, Trey, but I'm not a cheat. You want to cheat on some poor woman, don't bring me in on—"

"Hear me out. Please." He set his empty glass down on the table and noticed she hadn't taken more than a sip. "You going to finish that or what?"

"Depends on what you're going to tell me."

"Then you're probably going to need a double. First off, Natalie really doesn't exist. I made her up."

"Why'd you go and do a screwball thing like that?" Instinctively, she glanced at the kitchen doorway that led to the backyard, trying to calculate her chances of making it past him if she needed to. If this man was crazy, he was dangerously crazy.

"My mother's very ill."

"So she told me." She still didn't take another sip, preferring to wait and see what he was going to try to sell her next.

If it was a load of hogwash, she'd rather be sober enough to laugh it off.

"About six months ago she took a pretty bad turn. I really thought it was the end. She did, too. And you know what? She was less worried for herself than about not seeing me happy before she died. Happy with a woman, I mean."

"So you told her you had a girlfriend called Natalie?"

Embarrassment turned his skin two shades deeper. "Sounds stupid, I know, but—"

"Got that right." In her anger she was harsh. "Don't tell me Mr. Personality can't scrape up a real, live girlfriend on his own."

He lifted his hand and showed her his wedding ring—as though it wasn't already on her mind. "I loved my wife very much. When she died, she took my soul with her."

She softened a little at the enormity of his grief, but she had to point out, "That was a long time ago, Trey."

He folded his arms across his chest. Since he hadn't bothered to put his undershirt back on, she was treated to the bulge and ripple of his muscles. "That's what Mom says. She cut me some slack for three or four years, then started agitating. Why don't I start dating again? When am I going to find someone else? What about grandbabies?" He lifted his eyes to hers. "I don't want anyone else."

"I'm sure your mother isn't expecting you to get married right away or anything. But she'd at least like to know you're enjoying, uh, female company. That you're having a good time with the women that you date."

"What women?" His laugh was bitter, ironic.

So the Twilight Zone effect was still in play. "Let me get this straight. You haven't been on a date in six years?"

He shook his head.

"But you told your mother you had?"

"We thought she was dying," he repeated, as though that explained everything. "And she was so upset for me. I couldn't let her take that pain to her grave. So I made up a story. I told her I'd met this girl at a convention, and that I'd fallen in love."

"And she didn't ask to meet her before now?"

"I told her she was traveling. Out of state. That we were courting by phone."

Such an old-fashioned word, courting. "And she bought that?"

"She was so willing to believe it, she swallowed everything I said. Never mind that the story was so full of holes. Then I got the opportunity to move east and buy the travel agency. I knew she'd worry about my being alone, so I told her Natalie lived here, in Santa Amata. And I was moving to be with her."

"Stupid," she said, but not too unkindly. "Didn't you think you'd have to fess up sometime?"

"Not at first. Since she was so close to passing, I didn't really think about it. I'd say anything in such a state. I thought she'd slip away peacefully and never know the truth."

"But she got better."

"Hallelujah."

She felt a tenderness for him, and sympathy for his predicament. How could you not feel for a man willing to go to such lengths to protect his mother from hurt? Then she remembered she was now part of the whole big mess. She said resentfully, "And now you've gone and dragged me into it."

"I didn't drag you into anything, Kendra. You were there. It was happenstance. She caught us with our pants down—"

She was quick to interrupt. "Not exactly."

"Well, close enough," he conceded. "Let's just say it was bad timing. At least, ours was bad. Hers was worse."

The reference to their fevered entanglement in the narrow hallway made her itchy with embarrassment—and residual lust. She hoped he couldn't sense either. "So what happens now? How're you going to get yourself out of this?"

When he lifted those eyes to hers—those beautiful eyes—

she understood his unspoken plea, and threw up her hands before her. "Oh, no."

"Kendra…"

She ducked past him and headed for the back door, onto the patio where he planned to have barbecues—if he made any friends. "Oh no, no, no. I was on my way out when this whole thing went down. I'm on my way out now."

He grasped her by the wrist and twirled her around. "Kendra, please. It's only for two weeks. You heard her. She's leaving on a trip. Just two weeks."

"Two weeks of what? Letting you two call me Natalie? Pretending to be your ghost girlfriend? Are you nuts?"

"Maybe less, if I can get to the bottom of this fight with my father. Maybe I can convince her to go back to him. They have a wonderful marriage. It's just that Pops can be a little obtuse when it comes to women. I don't know what triggered this off, but whatever it is, she'll forgive him. She just needs to talk to someone."

"And what then? You going to continue with this lie long-distance?"

That thought didn't seem to have occurred to him. "As soon as I know she can handle it, I'm going to tell her. Everything. But I don't think she can take another shock to her system right now. The fight with Pops, this benighted trip to Egypt. Even the flight over here put her under strain. I don't think the time is right. She's had—"

"Two heart attacks. I know." She had every sympathy for Marlene's ailment, but it was turning into Trey's stock excuse for folly after folly. There had to be a point where he called a halt to the madness. She hopped off the deck and began to wade through the knee-high grass, trying to get to the front yard.

He caught up with her without even trying. "Where're you going?"

"Home, where I belong."

"Your purse is on the table back there," he pointed out.

She halted in her tracks. Way to ruin a great exit. But before she could turn to retrieve it, he caught her hand in his. Its warmth and firmness did a number on her resolve. "If going down on my knees and begging would help, I would."

She didn't think she could handle the intimacy of such a gesture. "Don't even think about it." She was angry, and surprisingly disappointed, to learn that this great, golden man was standing on clay feet. He'd lied like a dog to his mother for months, and he had the gall to act morally superior to her? She was thrown by her need to punish him, to get back at him for the humiliation he'd heaped upon her, by serving up some of her own.

"You're a liar."

"Yes," he admitted humbly.

"And you want to make me one, too."

He squeezed his eyes shut. "Sometimes circumstances…"

"Circumstances do what, Trey? Force you to cut a deal with 'someone like me'?"

He felt the brunt of his own words being thrown back in his face and winced. "I wouldn't ask if it wasn't—"

"You're a dishonest man. Problem is, you're too smug and self-satisfied to notice. You parade around your office, in your big glass tower, and humiliate me in front of people I've worked with for a year and a half. You wanted to fire me? Fine. But you could have had the decency to do it in private. After-hours."

He listened, ashamed.

"But no, the Big Chief wants everyone to know who's in charge. Who has the moral upper hand." She punctuated her point with a bitter laugh. "And now you want me to help you clean up a mess you created all on your lonesome? Oh no."

Her tirade gave him an idea. The pleading was over. The shame was gone. His face hardened, and he was all business. "Okay, how 'bout this? I clean up your mess, you clean up mine."

She gasped. "What?"

"Two weeks. That's all I'm asking for. Let me get my mother off on her way, back home to my father. I'll tell her the truth, once she's settled again. But in those two weeks, you're Natalie. We're a couple."

Was he deaf, or just so single-minded that nothing she said penetrated? "But I just told you—"

"In exchange, I clear your debt. Every penny. Fourteen thousand dollars is a lot of money, Kendra."

So tempting. So wrong. "You son of a—"

"It'd take a mighty long time to work it off otherwise. But if you take me up on my offer, in two weeks we'd be square. You can just walk away."

So, a new deal was on the table; one far worse than the first. At least that one involved hard, honest work. This one would place a strain upon her conscience she didn't think she could endure. "That's vile."

"It's business."

"Business, eh?" She was about to turn him down one final time, when she saw an opportunity, one so perfect that it could solve all her problems in a single stroke. She'd be a fool not to go for it. Her expression matched his. "Well, in business, people barter. You got more, and I want it."

His eyes opened wide, angry. "More than fourteen—"

"No, not money. Contrary to your opinion of me, it's not my be-all and end-all. I want my good name back."

He looked insultingly skeptical. "How d'you propose I do that?"

"You absolve me. You put the word out that you made a mistake. You had the wrong culprit. The money wasn't missing after all. However you want to play it." She made a gesture that showed how little she cared what method he chose. "You're a bright boy. You figure it out."

He examined her, contemplating. "I suppose I could…."

He was weakening, beginning to see things her way. While

the advantage was hers, she pressed harder. "And I want a letter of recommendation from you. I won't get another job otherwise." Stalemate. She waited.

She didn't have to wait long. He held out his hand. "I think I can live with that."

She shook and released his hand, almost sweating with relief—and foreboding. "Blood," she muttered.

"What's that?" He cocked his head, not sure he'd heard her right.

"Why do I get the feeling we should be signing this contract in blood?"

He laughed, charming again, now he was getting his own way. "Not until I unpack my horns and tail."

She was reluctant to join him in laughter, unable to shake off the feeling that, although on the surface she'd won, she'd dug herself a very deep hole indeed. Pretend to be his girlfriend? Turn up every day, join in on intimate family meals, let him treat her as though they were in love? Did she have what it took? If she didn't, she'd have to find it. She turned abruptly and headed back toward the living room.

He was right behind her. "Where're you doing?"

Wordlessly, she began unpacking his stuff, taking up right where they'd left off earlier.

He watched her for several moments, puzzled. "You don't have to work anymore. We have a deal, remember?"

She gave him ten long seconds to ponder the stupidity of his comment, and then said, "Would Natalie leave you to do all this unpacking alone?"

He got it. "Not if she loved me, she wouldn't."

She began unrolling an ornament wrapped in paper. "Well then."

Chapter 7

The Ship in the Bottle

By Thursday, Kendra had got the hang of the commute over to Trey's place. She discovered an alternative bus that shaved fifteen minutes off the trip, and although it didn't make much difference, given that she wasn't called upon to turn up exactly at eight anymore, she continued to do so as a matter of pride.

She walked up his path, taking pleasure in the scent of freshly cut grass. The birds were even happier now, as the low-cut grass made it easier to spot and pounce upon hapless bugs; those tired of that diet feasted at either of the two bird feeders he'd set up, although there they encountered competition from the squirrels, who couldn't believe their luck. Free food every morning, and a birdbath for cavorting in.

Trey greeted her at the door. Dressed for work, he was in danger of morphing from the barefooted Trey who'd kissed her into the cold, scary businessman who'd made her life miserable just over a week before. But the smile on his face nicely bridged the gap between the two. "Morning."

"Morning, Trey."

"Slept well?"

"Wonderfully, thanks." She eyed him skeptically. It was way too early in the morning to put up with this overdose of nice. Whatever he was up to, she didn't want to find out. She tilted her body a little to see Marlene hovering behind him, on the threshold of the front door, watching him greet her. "Morning, Marlene."

"Natalie! How nice to see you." She was always so warm and happy to see 'Natalie' that it was a shame. Kendra tried to match Marlene's smile with one just as broad. "Nice to see you, too, Marlene."

Standing a step below Trey, she felt shorter than she really was, especially since he towered over her when they were on level ground anyway. She wondered if he was going to let her by. He didn't move. Was there a secret password?

Marlene piped up. "What, son? You going to stand there staring, or you going to kiss her good morning? Don't be coy on my behalf. I'm not senile yet. I knew the way of the world before you were born, young man. If you want to kiss her, go ahead and kiss her!"

Over my dead—Kendra began to think, but he bent down from on high and kissed her lightly on the lips. It was a lucky thing she had good sea legs, or the shock of the quick contact would have sent her tumbling backward down the steps.

Not seeming to care that he'd sent her compass spinning on a frantic search for North, he grinned. "I was just admiring her for a minute."

Oh, you're good, she thought, when the horizon was once again a straight line. Someone would almost think you like me. Having kept their cover unblown for yet another day, he stepped aside and let her in. She hugged Marlene with real affection, feeling increasingly guilty that Marlene's returned affection was misplaced. At least, she consoled herself, hers was genuine.

"I think I'll hang around with you guys for a couple of minutes," Trey decided. "Have a quick bite before I head out."

As usual, Trey was attentive to both of them, pulling out their chairs and serving their meal. He loaded up his own plate with a mountain of bacon, flapjacks and syrup—thus tossing the whole notion of "a quick bite" into a cocked hat—and then sat between the two women with a sigh. "Big day today," he commented.

"Why?" Kendra asked.

"Got a supplier coming in to do a presentation on some Alaskan cruise packages. They're pricey, but if we could hammer out a deal that suits us both, it could be a really nice addition to the luxury lineup."

Kendra's ears pricked up. She'd been after Shel Salomon for months to consider an Alaskan package, but he'd been fixated on Caribbean destinations. People on vacation wanted to feel the sun on their backs, he insisted, not stare out over an ocean of glaciers. She was glad her idea was actually going to come to fruition, even if she wouldn't be around to see it. "That's nice," she said, with real enthusiasm.

Marlene wasn't as keen. "Oh, don't bore the child with work, Trey. The travel business might be fascinating to you, but not everybody understands it." She laughed. "Blackout days this, slow season that. Who can figure any of that out?"

"Oh, don't worry. I know what he's talking about. I'm a travel agent—"

"Are you?"

Too late, she realized her mistake. That was one heap of worms she wouldn't be able to coax back into the can. She cast Trey an anxious look, hoping he wouldn't be too ticked off by her gaffe.

He quelled her fears with a serene smile and stepped in. "Yes, Mom. That's how we met, remember? At a travel convention."

Oh, right. She'd forgotten that part of their bogus history. She tried to look as if she'd known it all along.

Marlene clapped her hands. "Oh, wonderful! You two couldn't get more compatible. I always say, if two people share the same interests, well, then they're halfway home. If your father was interested in half of what I did—"

Kendra expected Trey to seize the opportunity to bring up the whole pesky leaving-Dad issue, but he remained silent, allowing her to finish the thought—or not. She chose not. Marlene veered back on track as easily as she'd gone off it. "So, where d'you work? Not a rival agency, I hope. Trey's territorial, you know."

Ouch. "I'm, uh, between jobs right now."

"Between jobs? While your boyfriend owns a travel agency? That's ridiculous. I'm sure you're good at what you do. Trey, why don't you—"

He dropped the whole let-her-finish-the-thought strategy like a hot potato. "That's not possible, Mom."

"Why not?"

"Because…" He snared Kendra's eyes from across the table. She returned the challenge. *Get yourself out of this one, buddy.*

"Because it wouldn't be proper. I don't think the other employees would appreciate having the boss's…girlfriend…on staff. That could breed resentment." He added a little dig, "They might not trust her."

Couldn't resist that, could he? She launched a counterstrike. "Trust cuts two ways. Maybe if they knew how I got the job, the additional benefits that I provide…" She watched Marlene covertly; the woman was blissfully unaware of the undercurrents. "…They might not trust *you.*"

Touché, he conveyed silently.

Merci, she shot back. Then, wanting to keep Marlene out of the battle zone, she said, "Don't worry about me, Marlene. I'll be fine. I come with such a glowing recommendation that I'll have a new job in no time."

Trey couldn't resist a smile. "She's good at what she does, Mom. She'll do okay."

Marlene looked concerned and doubtful. "All right. If you say so."

"I promise."

She took her son at his word, and moved briskly on to other business. "Now tell me, sweet pea. When're you taking Natalie out?"

"We've been out three out of four nights, Mom."

"No, you two've taken *me* out. I mean, when're you two going out on your own? You don't need to put up with me every night, you know. Cutting into your couple time. Dragging along behind you like a bunch of old tin cans tied to the back of your car."

Kendra sensed what was coming and panicked. Go out alone? With Trey? She'd rather hang by her thumbs from the old apple tree in his backyard. "We enjoy your company. We love showing you around." She backed it up with a bright smile.

Marlene blew a raspberry. "Oh, bah! No need to humor me. I see the way you two look at each other when you think I'm not watching. I told you, I wasn't born yesterday. I know what coals look like when they're smoldering."

Smoldering? Her and Trey? Please.

Marlene waved her fork in her son's face. A chunk of Canadian bacon stuck on the tip was about to go flying. "Trey, take the girl out to dinner tonight. I'll stay home and watch TV. I'm tired anyway."

He was as reluctant as Kendra. "I'll stay with you, Mom."

When Marlene was being fierce, she looked more like her son than ever. "You do that, son, and I promise you I'll be blasting Paul Robeson and Johnny Mathis until one a.m. Oh, wait, I think I got some tapes with me of old Pastor Abraham's sermons. Remember him? He sure could talk. I hope your tape recorder still works, 'cause I feel like listening to a whole lotta church up in here tonight."

Trey grinned. "You got me there." He cocked his head to one side and looked at Kendra. "The alternative's starting to look mighty attractive."

Again, that sweet, anticipatory smile, as if he were genuinely enjoying the idea of being with her. Alone. On a date. For some odd, startling reason, she couldn't bear the knowledge that it was all an act. She looked away.

Marlene was grinning too, pleased with herself, now that she'd engineered the situation to her liking. She turned to Kendra. "Don't mind him. He's pretending he doesn't like church. But that's an old choirboy you got yourself there. Singing since he was seven."

Trey? Singing in a church choir?

"But let me tell you," Marlene went on, "I don't think he ever made it through a single sermon. Either he'd nod off, or somebody'd catch him with one of his little ships or airplanes hidden under his gown. Ask him how I used to smack the hide off him for embarrassing me like that in front of the pastor." Marlene lifted her eyes heavenward. "Oh, yes, old Pastor Abraham's tongue was blessed by the Lord. Gave some powerful sermons. Used to take us way past lunch. I'm aching to listen to a whole bunch of them tonight. How high do those speakers of yours go again?"

Trey reached over and took Kendra's hand. "Honey? Would you like to have dinner with me tonight?"

"And dancing," Marlene piped up.

"And dancing."

How'd she get herself into this? And how would she get out? Then, silly her, she remembered. This was all improv, remember? All she had to do was pretend to agree. Then Trey just had to stay out of the house for the rest of the evening, and come back and act like he'd been with her. She smiled. "I'd love to, *sweetheart*. If Marlene's sure she'll be okay alone, that is." She threw that lifeline in at the last minute, in case it proved useful later on.

"Marlene'll be hunky-dory," Marlene asserted. She looked like a cat with a mouse in its mouth and another holed up under the settee. "You can stay out late, too," she added significantly. "I can lock up tight, and make my own breakfast come morning."

Oh God. Was her face coloring up?

Trey didn't even go where his mother was trying to take them. He addressed himself to Kendra. "That settles it. What kind of cuisine d'you like?"

"You mean you don't know?" Marlene sounded puzzled.

Trey recovered smoothly from his gaffe. "I meant, what was she hankering for tonight?" He fished carefully. "Seafood? Thai?"

"Seafood's fine." She didn't care. She could have asked for nightingale's tongues, if she had a mind to. It wasn't like they were really going anywhere.

"Cool. I'll call up a few places and see what sounds good." He put his knife and fork down. To Kendra's relief, he announced, "That's it for me, ladies. I'd better get a move on."

Soon as he's gone, she told herself, I'll get going on the spare bedroom. Shouldn't take more than a day.

"Natalie," Trey began.

The spare bed had been broken down and shipped flat. Would she be able to set it back up on her own? Her thoughts were interrupted by a light touch on the shoulder. "Natalie?" His touch jolted her into her role again. She realized Marlene was listening, slightly confused.

"I'm sorry. I was thinking about the bedroom." Oh, trouble. "Your spare bedroom, I mean. Stuff I'm going to have to do today. You need a bedside rug. And your lamp, the blue one, got broken in transit. You need—"

"I was thinking you girls could take a break today. Go out, get some air. Just the two of you."

Without him as a buffer? Without work to focus on? Was he crazy? What if Marlene asked questions she couldn't answer?

But Marlene was all over it before she could find a good

excuse. "Wonderful! There's good shopping in Santa Amata, right? We could get you that lamp…."

Trey's response was swift and immediate. "Not a chance. I don't want you walking around, exerting yourself. Ken— Natalie will take you out to lunch, and then there's a concert on in De Menzes Park. A string quartet. You'd like that."

"I'd like shopping better," Marlene grumbled.

"You're going to the concert. I'm not having you brought back here by ambulance." He looked so school-masterish, Kendra had to choke back a laugh. He cajoled, "Come on, Mom. Have a girls' day out."

It wouldn't be so bad, Kendra reasoned. She liked Marlene. Maybe if she watched her tongue and remembered to respond to the name Natalie, she might get through this unscathed. "You'll have a good time," she said soothingly. "I'll make sure of it."

Trey took out his wallet and peeled off several bills from a fat wad and handed them to Kendra. She could have made a sarcastic comment about trusting her with his cash, but chose discretion over folly. She folded the money slowly and slipped it into her front jeans pocket. He leaned forward and kissed her on the forehead. "You two have a nice day," he said softly. Almost tenderly. Oh, he's good. He went around the table and kissed his mother in the same way. Before he could straighten up, she grasped his tie, holding him prisoner. "Trey…"

"Mom?"

"I saw that thing in your study."

He drew a deep breath. "What thing, Mom?"

"You know what thing. You know mighty well what thing. That ship. That hell-bound ship in the bottle."

He straightened up so sharply, Marlene was forced to let his tie go. "Leave it alone."

"I can't leave it alone. Why'd you bring it with you?"

"Because it's mine."

"Lord alone knows why you're so attached to that thing. It's cursed, and you cling to it. You bring it under a roof you plan to share with a new woman…"

"Mom…"

Kendra was so puzzled by the exchange she forgot to be embarrassed by the last statement. She watched the two as they argued, inordinately curious.

"….and bring a blight upon your own house."

Trey adjusted his tie, making sure it was straight again. "It's my home, and my bottle. I can do what I like with it."

"You give it pride of place? In the middle of your shelf, like it's a good thing?"

"Ashia wanted me to have it!" He raised his voice higher than he intended. Marlene looked shocked, but as determined not to back down as he was to drop it. His face was dark and tense with emotion, his eyes so black their centers were rimmed with just the thinnest circle of gray. He passed his hand over his head to calm himself down. "I'm sorry, Mom. I didn't mean to shout."

"I pray and pray that you'll see what I see, Trey."

"Mom, don't…"

"Get rid of it. Bury it. Burn it. It's only caused you heartache."

He stood there, his face working, striving to bring himself under control. Then he spun around and picked up his briefcase. He walked to the door. "That's the last conversation we'll have about this, Mom." He nodded at Kendra. "Take care of my mother for me."

"I will," she mumbled, but her mind churned. She was thrown back to her own mistake in picking up the ship, and his intense reaction. How could an innocent thing like a ship bring him heartache? What made it cursed?

The two women listened in silence to the sound of his car easing down the drive. Kendra was stunned, pained, wishing she could find a way to comfort Marlene after her son's blowup. But Marlene didn't look like someone in need of comfort.

Instead, she was examining Kendra's face closely, searching for something. Looking for a secret.

She's made me, Kendra thought. She knows I'm a fake.

"Natalie."

"Marlene?"

"Call us a cab. We're going shopping. Trey can hire a string quartet to play at my wake if he wants to, but for now I'm doing as I damn well please."

In the end, Kendra took her to Rosewood Mall, a sprawling shopping center outside upscale Belmont. As a compromise (and to deflect Trey's impending anger) Kendra had insisted they borrow an electric wheelchair. All shopped out now, they stood in a large atrium on the ground floor, wondering what to do next. They'd bought Trey a new rug and lamp, and a whole lot more. Kendra began to wonder if she was going to flag before Marlene did. "I think maybe we should sit for a while, Marlene."

"Oh, please. I haven't got all that long to live, remember? There's lots of shopping to do."

Faced with the prospect of another flurry of consumerism, Kendra decided to be honest. "If we don't sit soon, I'll probably go before you."

"Well, if you're tired, dear." Marlene looked around. "How about over there? I wouldn't mind a bit of Italian."

The restaurant was a pseudo-Italian affair called Little Sicily, complete with fake terrace and strung with garlands of garlic and peppers. The smell of sausages wafted through the doorway, making Kendra a little ill, but she was so relieved at the prospect of taking a break, she'd have gone for fast food. She wheeled the chair to a table near the entrance, where Marlene could amuse herself watching people come and go. They perused their vinyl-coated menus until a waiter came over. Beefy, dark-skinned and dreadlocked, he didn't look remotely Italian. He reeled off the specials in a thick Bahamian accent, putting any doubt about his possible Mediterranean ancestry to rest.

"Anything Alfredo will do," Marlene informed him with happy anticipation.

Kendra had something more like lean chicken and a salad in mind. "You sure all that fat's good for you?"

"What'll it do? Kill me?"

Kendra looked so stricken that Marlene patted her hand. "Don't worry, Natalie, dear. You sound just like Trey when you fuss like that."

"He's just worried about you because he loves you."

"I know. That's why I let him get away with bullying me."

Trey bullied Marlene? Kendra had good money that said it was the other way around. She tried to stifle a grin.

Marlene sighed elaborately. "But what can I do? He's my only child and I love him dearly."

They rifled through a basket of bread until their drinks came. Kendra was sipping on a cool melon concoction when Marlene came at her out of left field, "Do you?"

Her brain went blank. So did her face. "Do I what?"

"Love my son."

What to say? Lying for the sake of a sick woman's peace of mind was one thing. But to lie on love, to disgrace a concept she believed in deeply…that seemed so wrong.

She who hesitates is lost. This time, when Marlene took her hand, she didn't let it go. "You need to give it time. It's only been a few months for you two, right? And half of that's been long-distance. And it's been even longer since Trey had anyone in his life. I don't know if he's told you how long."

He had. She looked down at the strong hand closed over hers. "Six years."

"Six years is a long time. And for a man like Trey, who loves life so passionately, it's an eternity. That's why…" Marlene chose her words carefully. "…if he isn't as, um, demonstrative as you'd like, well, don't judge him too harshly. He'll come 'round."

The chances of Trey 'coming 'round' were near nil, but for Marlene's sake, she tried to agree. "I know."

Marlene suddenly looked so tired that Kendra felt a shard of panic. Had they overdone it? Trey would kill her.

"I wish… I just know, that if he'd let go a little, try to put the tragedy behind him, there'd be more room in his heart for you. He has a big heart, but it's so full of pain. And for the life of me, I'd swear he's aiming to keep it that way. Him and that bottle. That *bottle!*" She took her hand away from Kendra's and covered her face.

After a long time, Marlene looked up. There was wonder and discovery in her eyes. "You don't know about the bottle, do you."

"I've…seen it."

"But he hasn't…told you."

Told me *what,* she wanted to scream. "No."

Marlene sighed. "Oh, you poor baby." In a classic display of good timing, the waiter arrived. If he was anticipating the *ooohs* of delight he was used to when he set down their sizzling plates, he was disappointed. Neither felt like eating now. Marlene took out her midday pills and knocked them back with half her glass of water. She grimaced, and then said with purpose, "My son'll be mad at me for telling you this, but someone has to. He knows he should say something, but, well…"

"Tell me." Kendra was surprised at how keenly she wanted to know. She had no right to this information; it wasn't like she really was Trey's lover.

Marlene folded her hands on the table top and began. "My son married early. He was twenty-four, barely out of college, but so much in love with Ashia, it didn't matter. He always went straight for whatever he wanted. And he wanted her, from the moment he met her. His wife was a model, did he tell you that?"

She shook her head. She remembered the beauty in the photograph, the regal bearing, the sheer presence of the woman in Trey's arms. She wasn't surprised.

"She was from Somalia—born there, at least. She grew up in the States. Friends introduced them at a party. Oh, my, he was besotted. They moved in together two months later, never mind they were both just starting out and barely had a stick of furniture between them. They had each other, and that made them happy." Marlene began crumbling a breadstick into a pile on the red and green tablecloth. "They got married on Christmas Day that same year."

"Trey's birthday," Kendra remembered.

Marlene nodded. "It was good between them. Really good. She got pregnant four years later. Trey was the happiest man alive. Oh, you should have seen him."

"I wish I had," she murmured, surprised to find she wasn't just saying that to make Marlene feel better. The Trey Marlene was describing was so far from the shuttered man she knew. The only time he'd ever let his guard down in front of her, to make her suspect he was made of flesh and blood, was that day they'd kissed. She ached to hear more. "What happened?"

"What happened was that that blasted bottle killed her." Marlene leaned forward in a fit of coughing, placing her hand over her chest.

"Marlene!" Kendra leaped up and around the table to support her.

"I'm fine." She pushed her away and tried to pretend nothing was happening. "Go back to your seat."

"But you're sick. You're…"

"Please, Natalie. You need to hear this. You need to understand."

Against her better judgment, she sat. "Go on, then. But if you feel—"

"Stop fussing, honey child. Just listen." Marlene stared off into the distance. "It was Christmas. Of all the worst times. Trey had just got a job as assistant manager at a business consultancy. For the first time, they had money coming in, enough to see their way clear beyond the next paycheck. She was seven months along. Trey planned a big holiday celebration. He rented a chalet at Mammoth Mountain for a week. He flew over a day early to fix things up. You know? Decorations, lights. A Christmas tree. Ashia was on a shoot in southern California. Maternity wear. She was going to drive up the next day. It was a long drive. He wanted to go get her, but she wouldn't hear of it. He argued. She insisted. Well, you know what happened."

"She had an accident?" Kendra was almost scared to vocalize the thought.

Marlene nodded slowly, ruefully. "But it was worse. She simply didn't turn up on Christmas Eve, and by Christmas Day he was frantic. He called everybody but the national guard. She'd just disappeared. He drove that route all the way back to Malibu, and then back to the chalet again. Nothing. It was a road repair crew that found her car, two days after Christmas, in the bottom of a gully. Upside down. There was no way anybody could have seen it from the road."

"Oh," Kendra said softly, and added a silent *my God*. She felt Trey's pain as surely as if he were next to her, telling her his story himself. Or if he had somehow wormed his way into her head, her mind, her soul. She felt cold all over.

"It was hard to tell how long she'd lived after the crash, or if she was killed on impact. I still pray—I know the idea of retroactive prayer is ridiculous—but I pray she wasn't down there too long. Alive. Conscious. Missing my son and wishing…" Marlene drew a breath. "The car was full of presents. A layette for the baby. Holiday things. Happy stuff." Then the expression on her face curdled. "And then they found that thing."

"The ship in the bottle."

"Yes. That."

Marlene had said the ship had killed her. How? It stretched

Kendra's imagination to the limit. For the life of her, she couldn't imagine….

"See how old it is? It's a Civil War relic. Hand made by a Confederate sailor. It's a replica of the ship he served on. Ashia called me up a few days before to tell me she'd found it, and she was so excited. It was the perfect present." Marlene snorted.

Kendra couldn't take it any more. "But how did it…?"

Marlene looked as though it had never occurred to her that there could be any mystery about it. "The *brake,* girl. The police found it wedged under her brake pedal. They think she must have had it on the back seat with the rest of the presents, and it fell off and rolled under. They think something spooked her, an animal in the road, or maybe someone cut her off. She tried to stop and couldn't. And you want to know the kicker?"

"What?"

"The bottle didn't break. My poor daughter-in-law spent two days smashed up in a gully, with the life inside her belly gone, and that…*bottle*…didn't even get a crack on it. That's the Devil's mark for sure. And my son treats it like a holy relic." Tired from telling her awful story, Marlene closed her eyes and let her head fall into her hands.

Kendra leaned back, thoughts whirling. She'd learned more about Trey in five minutes from his mother than she had from the man himself in the time she'd known him. She could envisage Trey as a carefree young man, crazy in love with his stunning Somali bride. Building her a new home. Anticipating the birth of his child. She could imagine the pain and horror he must have felt at losing them both that way, and the sense of loss that burned in him after all these years. She was even willing to concede that an experience like that was enough to harden the warm, witty and passionate man she'd only glimpsed inside the cold, bitter man she knew. What she couldn't fathom was why in the name of all that was good, would he insist on keeping that thing?

"Understand now?" Marlene asked hesitantly. She looked afraid that she'd said too much, but hoped her revelations would at least make things easier for Trey and…Natalie.

Kendra did understand, just a little. Something nurturing in her made her long to reach out and soothe him. But that was stupid. He didn't even like her. What made her think he'd accept her comfort?

"Natalie?"

She became aware that Marlene was speaking again. She dragged herself out of her thoughts. "Yes?"

"I'm tired."

She wasn't the only one. "Me, too."

"And I'm not all that hungry, either. Besides, the food's gone cold."

They both looked down at their untouched plates, which were much less appetizing than they'd been when they were set before them. "Me neither."

"Maybe we could just…"

Kendra stood, placed a few bills on the table next to the full plates and grasped the handles of Marlene's wheelchair. "Loud and clear, Marlene. We can go home now."

Chapter 8

The Girl on the Fridge Door

There she was, naked as a porn star, studying her well-stocked wardrobe with a frown. Still hardly believing Trey truly was coming to get her. But he'd made it very clear this was to be no sham outing for the sake of fooling his mother. He really was taking her out, and he was due in fifteen minutes. The million-dollar question, then, was what to wear. He'd been nasty about her designer clothes, but he was just as scornful when she tried to avoid his comments by dressing down. So: label, or no label?

If she was going to be damned either way, she might was well please herself. She chose a pretty Vera Wang dress she'd picked up on Harbor Street, at the center of Santa Amata's clothing district. That place was practically her second home.

The white dress featured large, black, printed roses, with a fitted, sleeveless bodice, a plunging V-collar, matching belt and a pleated skirt that barely fell to the knee. The tops of her breasts were just visible and the skirt kicked saucily up as she walked, revealing her thighs.

She accessorized with pearl studs, a heavy silver ring, and an array of silver bangles. When it came to her feet, though, she wasn't compromising. Her Manolos were her Manolos, and if he didn't like them, too bad. She spun slowly in front of the full-length mirror, searching hard, as she did every day, for any sign that she was gaining her old weight back. She wasn't reed-thin, but she was holding steady at a weight she liked. She was quick to remind herself, though, that any relationship between the effort she was putting into looking fantastic and the fact she was going out with Trey was purely coincidental.

Now for the makeup. She was in a minimalist mood, going easy on the eyes and using a dab of blusher and lipstick—and then the buzzer went off. She froze, lipstick brush pressed against her pout. It took an effort not to glance again in the mirror as she walked to the door. Strangely eager, she opened it. He filled the doorway, looking way too good in a black leather jacket that was open at the front, revealing a stylish navy shirt. He had no tie, but platinum studs gleamed at his collar. His hair held its usual crisp wave and he was freshly shaven. Then she realized that he was sizing her up, too, and she let her curious gaze fall. Waiting for his verdict.

"You look lovely."

"Thanks." She let him in. His gaze swept the interior of her studio, examining her home with the same frank curiosity he'd used with her seconds before. As he looked around, she did, too, trying to see it through those expressive eyes of his. What she saw embarrassed her. It was way too small, she decided. Which was funny, since she'd always found it just right. The kitchen area was separated from the rest of the apartment by a break-fast table and two chairs, and opposite that was her unmade double bed. This month's issue of *Harper's* was open to an article on natural spa products, and the latest issue of *Vibe* was splayed on top of it. Her manicure kit was dangerously scattered about; leaping into bed right now would probably have resulted in a few lacerations.

Not that she was planning on leaping anywhere. She packed away the manicure tools, keeping an eye on Trey as his silent examination went on. The paint on the walls, peach trimmed with white, wasn't chipping, but it was a few shades lighter than it had been when it was fresh. Fortunately, much of it was obscured by pretty prints she'd picked up cheap, an original she'd bought off a street artist and a colorful silk scarf that she'd stuck to the wall with double-sided tape.

She stood with her back against a wall, hands clasped, feeling like she was at summer camp and the senior counselor was doing an unannounced dorm inspection.

He hesitated. "I hope you don't mind…."

"Not at all."

"I just…wanted to know who you are."

"And you think where I live will tell you?"

"Doesn't it usually?"

"Sometimes."

Something drew his attention to the photo of Fat Kat on the fridge door, and he walked over to it, squinting through the grainy window to her past. "Who's the girl? Your cousin?"

Why'd she leave the damn thing stuck up there? Tear it up; that's what she should have done. *Yes* would have been the easy answer, and then maybe he would have shrugged it off and moved on. But *yes* would have been a lie. "No," she mumbled. "Not exactly."

He glanced casually again, and then did a double take that would have been funny if the subject of it hadn't been her. "Is that you?"

Even from where she stood, she could clearly see the photo.

Or maybe the details were all etched into her memory. That ugly, ugly dress. The bird's nest of a hairdo; overprocessed, oversprayed and lank. Teeth that didn't even know what a straight line was. Skin that needed help but fast. The awkward girl in the photo hurt her heart.

She nodded. "It was." She waited for him to say something. Would he be patronizing? Mocking? Would he laugh out loud, or would she have to endure his pity?

Should have met him downstairs.

He took his time with the photo, brows drawn. Finally he said, "That's quite a transformation." Neutral. Diplomatic, even. But at least there was no laughter. He left the fridge and came close to her, concerned. "Am I making you uncomfortable? I didn't mean to embarrass you."

She squeezed out a laugh that didn't quite ring true. "That's okay. There isn't a teen in America who hasn't had an ugly prom photo taken."

He took her cue and laughed, too. "I had a six-inch hightop in mine. I looked like I'd wandered off the set of *House Party*." Then he added, "I don't think you were ugly, though. You were in your awkward stage. You just needed to grow into yourself."

"Or dwindle down *from* myself," she found herself saying. With him looking at the photo, Fat Kat looked fatter, geekier than ever. "The lady in the picture is my grandmother. She was my date for the prom. Nobody else asked me."

His voice was comforting, but not condescending. "Proms are overrated. A bunch of kids in overpriced clothes trying to sneak booze into a hall. Trying to act cool, trying to pretend they know how to dance, and trying to make it with kids they'll probably never see again once school's out."

"Maybe we know that now," she argued. She didn't want him to make it easy for her. "But back then, it was everything. The pretty girls, the popular girls, get asked. The ugly ones hang around with their backs to the wall and try not to get noticed. Wishing they could become invisible, like chameleons."

"Like you're doing right now?"

"What am I doing right now?"

"Standing with your back against the wall, wishing you could become invisible."

"I am not." She jerked her body away from the wall like it was on fire.

He took one last look at the picture, then faced her. "You don't need to."

"Don't need to what?" she asked suspiciously.

"Wish you could disappear," he explained. "You look beautiful."

Was he deaf? "I don't—"

"Even though you're missing a lip." He was smiling.

Eh? "I what?"

"You've got lipstick on your top lip, but none on your bottom lip. Is that how you ladies are wearing it these days?"

She clapped her hand to her mouth, ruining what lipstick there was in the first place. "Oh my God, Trey, why didn't you say something? I was putting my makeup on when you got here, and—" She raced around to the mirror, grabbed her lipstick, and fixed the problem. "Ready," she announced, a little out of breath.

He didn't move. He was standing before her, rock steady, taking in her clothes, her hair, examining her face so seriously she was sure she'd made another critical cosmetic error. Self-consciously, she touched her face. "Am I…"

"Costs quite a bit, doesn't it," he murmured. There was a look of revelation on his face, as if dawn was breaking.

She didn't get it. "What?"

"Recreating a whole new you. New body, new hair…"

God, she groaned inside. Not now.

"Dental work. Fine clothes, jewelry. Stuff to make you forget…."

Her legs went wobbly, giving out under her. She stumbled blindly toward the bed, and sat heavily on it. Why'd he want to go there? Why'd he want to dredge up her shame again? She put her hands over her face, bangles clacking. "Please, don't ask me…"

"That's why you did what you did, isn't it?" The bed sank as he sat beside her, the heat from his body radiating toward hers. "It's why you took the money."

There was no denying it. There could be no lies. All she could do was let it all pour out of her, a cleansing truth, and beg him to forgive. "I left Indiana to get away from me. I'd lost all the weight, through diet and exercise and expensive trainers. I was working on the…other things. But when I got here, I was still the same person." She sighed heavily, misery making her breath catch. "I needed a disguise."

"And you started buying pretty things."

She nodded, face still hidden by her hands. Unable to look at him.

"Why didn't you stop? When the bills started coming, why didn't you—"

"I couldn't! I wanted to, but…" She trailed off. It sounded so stupid when she laid it out like that. There was no way she could explain the panic she felt when she tried to put a halt to her compulsion. The unbearable fear that if she let her polished veneer slip just for a moment, Fat Kat would come back. "I wish you could understand."

"I'm trying," he said softly.

She held out her hands, fingers spread, begging him to believe her. "I was going to pay it back, Trey, honest. Soon as I could."

"How? Were you going to go to the accountant and hand over some cash, and say "Here, I stole this and I'm making good on it?"

"Borrowed. Not stole. And no, I didn't have a plan for putting it back, but as God is my witness, I was going to." She sneaked a peek at him. His face was unreadable. She spoke slowly and carefully, hoping that her intensity would convey the sincerity she felt. "I never meant to hurt Shel, or you. I… am…not…a bad person."

To her humiliation, she felt tears begin to burn. She rubbed them in irritation. She didn't need to become unbuckled in front of this man. Gently, he lifted a lock of hair away from her wet cheeks. "I know you aren't."

His kindness only made her feel worse. It only underlined her profound shame and despair. She brushed his hand away. "Why d'you care, anyway?"

The question made him pause. "I don't know…but…I care." He touched her face again. This time she didn't resist.

After several seconds he pulled away, looking almost surprised at his gesture, as if he hadn't meant to be as expressive as he'd been. He stood up and offered her a hand. "Come. Why don't we get out of here? We've got a reservation."

In a haze, she found her bag, her heart thudding, and walked outside beside him. After her revelation, she felt lighter, as if a stone had been lifted from her chest; but she had the feeling there'd be more hurdles to leap over tonight. This was a *date* date. With Trey. They'd be alone in a darkened room, sharing good food and wine. The idea both excited and frightened her.

She sat beside him in the car, every molecule in her body fighting not to convey her nervousness. It's only a few hours, she told herself. Then she'd be back home at her apartment. Safe. Alone.

His voice cut in on her whirling thoughts. "Can I ask you a personal question?"

Not too personal, she thought. It's scary, the idea of him knowing her. But she gave the polite answer. "Go ahead."

"You said your grandmother took you to prom. Why didn't your mother do it?"

"Because she wasn't there."

"She died?"

"I don't know. I've never met her. She had me at seventeen. She dropped me off with my grandmother and went to be with her boyfriend. My father. An older guy who'd taken up a new job in Indianapolis. She promised she'd be back to get me in a few months, when things got better." Kendra tried not to sound bitter. "I guess things never got better. She sent me presents, my grandmother said, for a few years. Then my father left her. Don't know much about what she did after that. The presents stopped coming."

"I'm sorry."

"It's okay. I dealt with it."

"That why you overate? To compensate for the loneliness?"

She was jarred by the frankness of the question, but not offended. "Probably. Yes. It took a long time…years…for me to understand the hole in my life didn't need to be filled with food. I learned to manage my eating by managing my emotions. Wasn't easy, but it worked. It took two years for me to get down to this weight."

"And you've kept it off."

"Yes." She was proud to tell him.

"Ever fall off the wagon?"

She shrugged. "I still eat when I'm upset. Angry, nervous, scared." She threw him a sidelong look. "I eat when I get fired."

He took that one in good humor. "How much weight did you lose?"

"Seventy pounds." There was a mixture of pride and embarrassment in the way she said it. "How d'you know so much about eating disorders?"

He laughed. "I was married to a model, remember? And models have model friends. If I had a buck for every rail-thin woman who moaned over my dinner table about the tragedy of gaining three pounds! Hate to say it, but Ashia's friends weren't a very stable bunch. They had ways of getting rid of food they've already eaten that would raise your hair."

"Really?"

"Mmm-hmm. I've known bulimics, anorexics and everything in between. When you're surrounded by a bunch of women who do nothing all day but take turns obsessing, there's only one thing a husband can do, sit quietly and listen. Informative. Not pretty, but informative."

It wasn't often that he shared that part of his life with her. She was openly curious. "And Ash...your wife?" That beautiful, willowy woman hadn't had a problem, had she?

"Oh, she did her share of crash dieting before a shoot. Living on diet colas and grapefruit for a day or two. But she never had a problem. She was naturally thin."

"Lucky her." This goddess had been so blessed for so much of her life. A dream job, a perfect figure, a besotted, gorgeous husband and the ability to eat without fear. If it hadn't been for the woman's tragic end, Kendra would have been jealous.

He glanced at her to see if she was being bitter or sarcastic, but satisfied himself that she wasn't.

Then they were outside the Aegean Isles, a swanky new Greek restaurant Kendra had been dying to try. Its whitewashed walls were festooned with mosaics of seahorses and porpoises made of pebbles, colored sand and shells, and lit by a soft blue glow. Rampaging green foliage swept down from the roof and crawled up from the ground. Water shimmered in small pools, and underwater floodlights sent ripples dancing across the building. He pulled to the curb. "I'm proud of you."

Now the ripples of light were moving through her, too. The way he looked at her made her excruciatingly aware of the smallness of the interior of the car. They were very close and very alone. The last time they were this close, a whole bunch of stuff that shouldn't have happened, had.

"Am I making you nervous?"

Shrewd. She tried to laugh it off. "A little. You'd better watch out. I might eat you into one heck of a dinner bill."

"That's okay," he joked back. "I brought my backup credit card."

"Good. I hope there's whale on the menu."

He unlocked the doors, but neither of them budged. "You don't need to, you know."

"Don't need to what?"

"Make jokes about your weight. Or be afraid. Of me."

She could come clean and admit she was floundering in her own sweat, or she could lie like a rug. She fought fire with fire. "Are you?"

"Am I…?"

"Afraid of *me*." She tried to make the question light, flippant, almost flirtatious, but it just didn't turn out that way.

He leaned back against his seat and closed his eyes, his face so intense that he seemed to be screening a home movie on the inside of his lids. She waited for an answer, afraid it would be positive, afraid it would be negative.

"Yes, I guess. A little."

This huge, strong, confident-to-the-point-of-arrogant man, afraid. Of *her*. Mind-blowing.

"Why?"

"Because this is new. Being out with a woman…on a date. It's been an awful—"

"Long time. I know." Again, compassion assailed her. As recently as this morning, she'd found it slightly ridiculous that he could shut himself off from female company for such a long time. But having heard Marlene's story, she understood. She only had words to comfort him with, though. Trying to do it with touch was too scary.

"It's no big deal," she tried to reassure him, but even she wasn't convinced. "It's just dinner between…friends."

He opened his eyes. If she fell into those dark gray wells, she'd drown. "No, it isn't. You know that. You've felt it all week, just like me."

She wouldn't insult his intelligence by denying it. "Nothing has to…happen."

He laughed softly, not believing her.

Time to cut your losses, Kendra. "You're right. This whole thing—dinner, dancing—maybe it's too much." Too intimate would have been a better way to put it. In non-verbal acknowledgment of her words, he threw the car into gear and pulled away from the curb. The door locks clicked back into place, sealing them off from the world again. She felt a sinking in her belly. As much as she understood why he couldn't go through with their date, she hated the thought of returning home. She'd protested against going out with him tonight; he had, too. But now that it was being taken from her, her disappointment was like a fresh paper cut.

She realized she was hungry. Genuinely hungry, not the vague longing inside her being that she habitually assuaged with food. She remembered she and Marlene hadn't been able to eat their lunch. As she watched the blue glow of the Aegean Isles disappear in the distance, filled with all the delights she wasn't getting to sample, she consoled herself. There was always eggs and toast. She'd cook up a whole mess of them once she was safe behind her locked doors.

The only thing that filled the void between them was the music that oozed from his speakers. Norah Jones's voice was the living expression of Kendra's own longing. She let her head fall sideways against the cool glass and watched her breath mist. Then he touched her, lightly. Hand upon the crisp black and white linen of her skirt, resting upon her thigh. His hand was so large that it obliterated one of the oversized print roses. Shocked, she glanced at him, but his eyes were fixed on the road. Did his left hand have a clue what his right hand was doing? She was afraid that if she moved a muscle or breathed a word he would take his hand away. So she kept silence like a World War II submarine on the ocean floor.

She tried to see past the misted-up window, seeking out landmarks. Anything to distract her from the warmth infusing her thigh—and everything that lay adjacent. But something wasn't right. He was heading east, rather than north to her place. "Trey, this isn't the way home."

He smiled. There was a glint of mischief there. "I didn't say we were going home. I agreed that we didn't have to do the dinner and dancing thing. Doesn't mean I'm ready to go home yet."

Oh, praise all the angels, he wasn't cutting their date short after all. She'd have more time alone with him, and more time to soak up the ripples of sensation his motionless hand was sending through her. Steady on, though. Don't let on how happy this makes you. She hit just the right note of levity. "Good decision. Your mom'd have killed you."

He shook his head. "This is not about her. Give up the chance to spend some time alone with a beautiful woman? *I'd* have killed me."

And so he left her, puzzling over the twin mysteries of his statement and their destination. It was a full ten minutes, with nothing between them but more Norah, before she figured out where he was taking her. He had to be joking. "Trey!"

"Yep?"

"You kidding me?"

His teeth flashed in the darkness. "Nope." The car sailed into the parking lot of Sycamore Park, Santa Amata's modest amusement park. Six Flags it was not, but it boasted an arcade, a midway and a few moderately scary rides. Kendra had only visited once. She gaped. "You're taking me to an amusement park?"

"Guess so. I heard about this place at the office, and had a hankering to visit. I just didn't want to do it alone. But rumor has it you're not doing anything tonight, so…"

"But I'm wearing a short skirt. And high heels."

"So walk carefully. And I promise I'll drape my jacket over your knees when we're up on the Ferris wheel." He slid into a parking spot, pulled up the parking brake and shut off the engine, letting her know conclusively that her protests were falling on deaf ears. He hopped out, came around and opened her door.

She got out, protesting even as she did so. "Sycamore Park? This is crazy! What got onto you? It's the last place I'd have expected you'd want to see. It's so unlike—" She caught herself in time, vaguely aware that the observation was a tad insulting.

He was onto her anyway. "Unlike me?" He took her jacket from her hands and swung it around her shoulders, but instead of stepping back, he let his hands rest on her upper arms—tossing her into a windstorm of déjà vu. He was so close she could feel the seductive warmth emanating from him. She could smell the leather of his jacket. "I wasn't always such a humorless bastard," he told her.

A polite protest would be pointless. She shut up and listened.

"I used to be fun at parties. I had friends. We shot hoops and drank beer on Fridays after work. I used to be impulsive, get up and go somewhere just because I thought it would be fun. I used to be good…company." His eyes weren't holding hers, as she'd thought they would be. They were focused on her mouth.

She tried to wet her lips, but her mouth had gone dry.

"That's not the confusing part. I know why I am the way I am. The confusing part is, there's something about you that makes me want to be…" He searched for a way to express himself. "…the man I was before."

If she'd had a mind to answer him—and God knew what she could possibly have said to that—she didn't have the chance to do so. Because all she could feel was his mouth on hers.

The last time he'd kissed her there'd been passion and rage and pent-up wanting. This time, it was sweet and searching, hesitant, almost as if he was puzzled by his desire. There'd been that familiar, early evening springtime chill in the air when she'd gotten out of the car, but now his kiss chased it away.

He stopped and pulled back, and stood looking down at her.

She hoped he didn't expect her to say something. She was too busy digesting what *he'd* said to *her*. Then he shrugged his jacket closer around himself, pocketed his keys, and jerked his head in the direction of the main entrance to the park. "You in?"

She nodded. He looked satisfied, offering his arm. But as he led her to the ticket office, she was filled with lingering doubt. What, exactly, was she "in" for?

"Call a lawyer," she yelled. "I've got whiplash!"

"Sue me," he mouthed from across the way.

"I'm thinking about it," she mouthed back. She hadn't been paying attention, and he'd sneaked up on her from behind and crashed into her, sending her reeling. Worse, he was laughing as he did it. She wrestled with the steering wheel of her red and silver bumper car, spun out in an arc and went at him head-on. She meant business. When he'd humiliated her in the shooting gallery, she'd chalked it up to superior masculine hand-eye co-ordination. He was a faster molewhacker than she was, and she let that one pass, too. Bigger biceps, all right? But then there were the slot machines, where he'd made out like a bandit, cashing in almost fifty bucks after only twenty minutes. And he'd managed to knock over a whole bunch of milk bottles, even though they both knew they were rigged.

But now he didn't have his physical strength to rely on, and the playing field was level. It was all machine against machine, driving skill against driving skill, and she wasn't going home without having tasted victory at least once. He wanted a war? Bring it, baby. She floored it, slamming into his left flank at a speed slightly above the manufacturer's recommendations. He grunted, but before he could rally, she smashed into him again, backing him into a corner where she could pummel him at her leisure. When she was tired, she let up, hollering in victory like a Hun on a rampage.

When she helped him out of the car they were both laughing.

Maybe he'd let her win. She didn't mind. The good thrashing gave her an outlet for some of the resentment she'd been holding against him. They staggered away, hanging onto each other, trying to find both their balance and their breath.

"Oh God, Forrest, you were a wildwoman back there."

"You deserved it."

"I deserved to get beaten on like a punching bag at a gym?"

"You did." She remembered those first few days home alone after he'd ousted her without ceremony, when she'd whiled away many an hour dreaming up every nasty thing she could do to him, from voodoo dolls right on back. Bumper cars hadn't come to mind then, but they sure had done the trick. She gave a villainous cackle.

He shook his head ruefully, rubbing his hip. "I'm glad you got your jollies, but I hope you still think it was worth it when I wind up in traction."

"Oh, it'll still be worth it."

His arm slipped casually around her waist, sending jolts zinging through her. "What now?"

"You asking me? I thought the alpha male was calling the shots tonight."

"Alpha male feels like he's been busted all the way down to gamma. Maybe we should do something quieter."

"Quieter? At Sycamore Park? Even the mannequins are rowdy."

"We'll find something." He searched around for a good prospect. "Want anything more to eat?"

"Are you kidding?" They'd had corn dogs and candied apples, New York–style pizza, saltwater taffy and warm sodas, and still she'd managed to take a few spins on the Ferris wheel ride without throwing up. Eating anything else would be begging for trouble.

"Just checking."

"I can't even slide a nacho in sideways."

"Good. Let's see what more there is to do around here, then." He brightened. "Ah, that looks like just the ticket."

"What?"

He dragged her across the midway to a ride called "Mississippi Mayhem." It promised a slow, looping trip on a rickety, open-air caboose that delved underground in a weird combination of Tunnel of Love and Horror House.

"You game?"

"You challenging me?"

"I could be."

"Then, yeah, I'm game." She hopped into a faded yellow seat without waiting on him to assist her. He slid in beside her. The seat belts were frayed and unusable, but they weren't necessary anyway; if they made it to a speed of ten miles per hour, they'd be doing plenty. The train lurched, groaned, thought hard about setting off, and eventually did. The ride was as hokey as it could get. Grungy taverns on the banks of the "river" were peopled by mannequins partying to the tinny sound of piped jazz. A riverboat's wheels wobbled in the blue-painted wooden cutout waves that jerked back and forth on gears, as folks onboard gambled, drank and fought.

"Unbelievable," he remarked. "This ride is older than I am." He pointed excitedly. "Did you see that?"

"What?" She couldn't see a darned thing in this darkness.

"I didn't know spiders got that big so far north of the Equator."

She shrieked. "What?"

Now it was his turn to laugh. "Relax. It was probably rubber."

"It better be," she said fervently.

"I'll tell you something else about that spider."

She watched him suspiciously. "Please do."

"If it's alive and has a hankering for human flesh, you'd better watch your butt, baby, because we're the only ones on the menu."

He was right. They were the only couple on the ride. "Should we chalk that up to the fact that it's the middle of the week, or is it that nobody's here because this is quite possibly the worst amusement park ride on the East Coast?"

"Haven't a clue. But I know one thing."

"I'm afraid to ask."

As he leaned forward, the caboose swayed. His face was inches from hers—and not a whole lot of inches at that. "If I let this opportunity pass, they're gonna have to revoke my man license."

She was bemused, but smiling. "Huh?"

"If I have a fair maiden in my clutches, and we're in a quiet, dark place, with no eyes on us—"

"Spiders have, like, *lots* of eyes," she reminded him.

"Not the rubber ones," he retorted. "And you're interrupting my spiel."

God, his jacket smelled so good she wanted to bury her face in it and inhale. She knew from experience he smelled even better. She narrowed the already narrow gap between them. "Sorry. Continue."

"As I was saying, if I let this opportunity slip me by, if I don't walk away from this with so much as a kiss, well, I'm no man at all."

"You're plenty man," she asserted with feeling.

"You make me feel like plenty more."

Their kiss lasted longer than the ride, so when the train panted back to the surface, Trey lifted his head and he looked at her enquiringly. She nodded. Barely glancing at the grinning kid who was running the monstrosity, he handed over a strip of tickets, all he had left, buying them a few more revolutions on Ole Man River.

Underground again, he pulled her roughly onto his lap so she was facing him, straddling his thighs. She was glad now for the short skirt; it made it easy to slip her legs around him. The stale air, the dust, the asthmatic rasp of the gears as the train dragged along, meant nothing to her. All she could smell was warm skin, leather and cologne. All she could hear was the sound of his voice as he murmured soft, inconsequential things.

The ripple of his hair under her hands reminded her of the reflections of light on the wall of the restaurant they'd shied away from. Afraid to be alone together—had they been nuts? Round and round they went, and with each revolution she grew more excruciatingly aware of him. One of his hands was around her waist, the other had ventured under her skirt. Driving her stark raving loony. His lips tasted like strange fruit. He made her mouth water.

"Trey." She didn't even know why she was calling his name.

But he did. They still had two, three rides left, easy; but they'd both had enough. The next time they looked up and saw the starry night, he took her hand and helped her up. "I think it's time to get out of here," he said softly.

She stepped out of the train and onto terra firma, but she was still giddy. Nervous. No, not nervous. Nervous was for piano recitals, or your first day at kindergarten. She was flat-out scared. Now was the time to talk, tell him they'd be making a mistake. But if this was a mistake, well, she was willing to pay the price, whatever it was.

There was nothing left for either of them to say. They walked side by side back to the car, her hip brushing his. She was glad for the uneven paving in the parking lot. Having to focus on not getting her heels stuck in one of the cracks gave her something to think about. Something other than him.

They drove back to her apartment, each wrapped in their own thoughts. Norah Jones serenaded them, set the mood. When he parked outside her place, she invited him in, sealing her fate, and his. He brought the CD with him.

Chapter 9

Safe Harbor

Trey stood just inside the door as she locked it. When he'd come to pick her up, she'd worried about what he'd think of the place, whether it looked tiny or shabby to him. Now, all she could think about was the largest piece of furniture there: the bed.

"Something to drink?" she asked as a matter of form. "Coffee? Or, if you feel like it, I think I have something stronger somewhere." She looked around as if she expected to find a bottle of triple malt poking out of her potted fern.

He was solemn. "No, thank you. I'm fine."

No use pretending that she was just inviting him in for coffee. They both knew what they were there for. She only wished he didn't look so stunned, shell-shocked, nervous. Music. That'd help. She took the CD from his unresisting fingers and slipped it into her small player. The sound quality didn't come close to that of the sophisticated system in his car, but she didn't care. She went back over to where he was standing. "It's okay, you know," she told him.

He shook his head, but she wasn't sure if he was negating her assertion or simply trying to clear his thoughts. She went to him with her arms outstretched, but instead of taking him into them, she helped him out of his jacket and then concentrated on undoing the buttons of his shirt. He was as compliant as a small boy being undressed for beddy-byes by the sitter.

She undid his belt buckle, a ribbon of calm weaving its way through her. When his shirt and pants were off, she folded them carefully and laid them over the back of a chair.

"Trey."

"Yes?"

"Come with me." She took his hand and led him to her bed. The sheets were askew and the small pile of glossy magazines was still there, but none of that mattered. She kicked off her shoes and slipped out of her pretty black and white dress.

Wearing only their underwear, they faced each other. He reached for her like a blind man feeling in the dark for a way out.

Why was it that every time she kissed this man, it was different? This time, there was an urgency that threatened to suck her down. He pressed against her, feeling bare female skin against his for the first time in years. He kissed her mouth like he'd forgotten what a woman tasted like. He inhaled the scent of her skin and hair.

She reached up, took his glasses off and set them down on the bedside table. Then he held her against him, lifting her so that her feet were a few inches off the floor. I'm too heavy, I'm too heavy, she was thinking, but he held her with ease, and it felt so good. She kept her peace.

"I hope I don't…disappoint you," he murmured against her skin.

Disappoint her? This incredibly gorgeous, physically

flawless man, fully aroused, filled with desire for her—for *her!* This puzzle of a man, at once infuriating and obnoxious, tender and sweet, urgently pressing against her, communicating with his body how much he wanted her. Her own body answering, letting him know in return that she wanted him so much that if she did not have him right now, tonight, she would lose her mind. There was no way he could disappoint her.

She needed to tell him that. "You could never—"

"I'm not even sure I remember—"

"You remember. You just pushed it so far into the back of your mind you think you've forgotten." She snaked her hand down his belly and into the waistband of his shorts to stroke him lightly. His whole body quivered, and a hiss escaped his clenched teeth. "See? Your body remembers."

They tumbled onto the bed, kissing as urgently as they had in that rickety train back at the amusement park. If he'd forgotten, it was all coming back to him. He unhooked her bra without a fumble, and pulled the straps down her arms. It got lost among the rumpled sheets. He let his hands roam over her breasts. They moved in circles and swoops, as if he was spreading warm oil over them, smoothing it into her skin. She inhaled sharply.

His hands were on her hips, fingers hooked into the waistband of her black panties. They didn't exactly match her bra, but that was okay, too. "Up," he instructed softly.

She lifted her hips, allowing him to slide the wisp of fabric down her thighs and off her completely. Now she was bare to him, all one-hundred-thirty-odd pounds of her, and he was looking at her like she was the Queen of the Nile.

He lowered his head and pressed his lips against the upside-down bowl of her belly, leaving trails of intense sensation as he swept back and forth. No matter where he went on his journey of exploration, he returned to the hub of her navel to dip his tongue into it.

But she was being greedy. Selfish. He needed this more than

she did. So she took charge, rising up and coaxing him down onto his back so she could minister to him as he'd ministered to her. His shorts joined hers on the bed, or the floor, or wherever.

Oh, man. He was un-be-*leivable*. Gorgeous, flawless, a study in beaten bronze. She brushed her lips against his belly, as he had done, and heard his breath catch. She inched lower, noticing that his pubic hair was the same dark sable as that on his head. The scent that emanated from him made her drunk.

The taste of him was an explosion. He was a medley of soft, fine skin, raw, masculine scent and sweet-salt nectar. He jerked as she engulfed him in her hot mouth, fingers burying themselves in her hair, as if he was undecided whether to draw her closer or push her away. He was hard, hot and delectable. She feasted on him until she knew he wouldn't be able to bear it a single second more, and then she lifted her head. Those gray eyes were huge and black with hunger, as round as twin moons.

The condoms in her medicine cabinet were so thin and light you could forget they were there. She was back with them in her hand before he even missed her. She threw a leg across his hips and clambered onto him, squeezing her eyes shut and trying to keep from shouting out as he grasped her hips and thrust himself up into her.

Throughout the battle that followed, he didn't say a word. Barely a moan escaped him. They were shipwrecked on a sea of silence, clinging to each other to stay afloat. This silence was something Kendra had never experienced before. She'd had lovers who were reduced to baby talk, lovers who kept up a running commentary, like radio coverage of a baseball game, and lovers whose conversation got a little too down and dirty for her liking, but this silence—this was new. She felt intimidated enough to guard her own tongue, even though she wanted to gasp out her pleasure.

Because there *was* pleasure, an almost intolerable level of it. His body *did* remember. Instinct overcame insecurity and doubt. She was overwhelmed by the sheer power of his physique, the weight of him, the density of muscle and bone. She was startled by his intensity; he delved into her, ate her up like he was starving. When he'd had enough of allowing her to lead, he flipped her onto her back, taking charge.

But too soon, even as she was pressing back against him, matching him stroke for stroke, seeking her own fulfillment, she felt an earthquake rumble through him. He gritted his teeth, as though willing it to stop. Trying to hold back. But sometimes the body is master of the heart and mind, and his body knew what it wanted. He broke his silence in an agonized cry, and then went limp upon her as the life force drained out of him.

She put her arms across his back, feeling his chest heave. Her breasts were flattened against his ribs, and she had to fight for her breath even as he struggled for his. He recognized her discomfort and eased off her, rolling onto his back. His sticky skin was still pressed against hers, giving her warmth and reassurance.

"I'm sorry," he said.

"I'm not." They'd fallen upon each other with hunger, and she'd fed upon the pleasure he'd given her with every touch and every stroke. She was content; to want anything more would be greedy. She shifted, turning onto her side so she could lay her head against his shoulder, place her arm across his chest, and observe him as the world slowed down upon its axis.

His heat-blackened eyes were wide open and focused on something in the vicinity of her ceiling. He blinked as if blinking back tears, but none came. Although they were still skin-to-skin, she felt like there was a wall between them. A barrier so dense and insurmountable that she couldn't tell for sure if he was still aware that she was there. He shifted a little, bringing his right hand across himself to caress the thin gold band on his left. He did so lightly, almost as if he wasn't consciously aware of the gesture, but it told her all she needed to know.

Kendra felt a chill, the kind she'd read about in horror

stories, the one that signaled the presence of a ghost. Ashia was here. If not as a genuine manifestation, then as a memory so real for Trey that her presence was tangible.

There he was, haunted by the spirit of his beautiful wife, and there she was, taunted by the memory of Fat Kat. There were too many people in this bed.

There would soon be one less.

She felt the bed dip as Trey rose. She watched him, filled with melancholy and helplessness as he got dressed. She should say something, shouldn't she? But what? *Stay the night, please? Are you sad? Are you mad? Do you wish you hadn't?* And even if she did ask, would he answer? They'd leaped together into a pit of silence that was so wide it had no edges, and so deep it had no floor. How could she even try to claw her way out of that?

He found his glasses and put them on, and then looked at her like she was only now coming into focus.

Say something, she willed him. *Anything.*

Talk to me!

He leaned forward, but his eyes did not connect with hers. He kissed her lightly on her forehead and let himself out.

Kendra hadn't expected to sleep so soundly, sure her unsettled mind would keep her awake. But good loving took its toll. She'd flaked out within minutes of Trey's departure.

She woke up smelling of him. She lingered awhile amongst rumpled sheets, enjoying her body's memories of their commingling. But in spite of her pleasant languor, her mind was filled with perplexing, contradictory thoughts. Sleeping with Trey had opened up a Pandora's Box of emotions: overwhelming new feelings for him; affection—more than affection. Desire, curiosity, jealousy over his loyalty to his long-dead wife. Most of all, she felt worry over how guilty he felt. He'd left like a whipped dog, his tail between his legs, penitent, ashamed.

Part of her understood and was sympathetic. It couldn't have been easy for him to break a vow of celibacy. To venture into the turbulent waters of sex after having spent so many years stranded on the rocky shore staring out at the horizon. Part of her felt his pain and longed to comfort him in any way she could.

And part of her was nail-spittin' mad.

What'd he think this was? A game? What kind of man got up from a woman's bed and walked out without so much as a word? Even call girls got a muttered "thank you" as the front door slammed. Her umbrage provided enough fuel for her to leap out of bed and stomp to the shower. She was so angry she was sure she heard the water hiss as it hit her body, fogging the glass doors in self-righteous steam.

She wasn't obliged to his place this morning, but she'd promised she'd be there. It was what Marlene would expect of Natalie. Much as she'd have liked to lie low and avoid the man until she could get her feelings back under control, she was going over there. And soon as they had a moment alone, Silent Bob was going to get a piece of her mind.

By the time she made it to his place, her ire had cooled a little, and she was half-hoping he'd already left for work so she wouldn't have to go through that awkward morning-after ballet.

Wrong. Even if his car hadn't been parked in the garage, she'd have known he was there the second she stepped into the house. His energy was so huge that it announced his presence before she heard him speak. The bottom fell out of her stomach.

Two voices rang out through the house, both sounding too emphatic for Trey and Marlene to be having an ordinary conversation. She entered via the unlocked front door and passed through the living room, but stopped at the kitchen, feeling awkward and intrusive. Maybe she should just back out again....

Trey spotted her, and that was the end of that. "Hey," he called softly. He looked at her like he was touching her face.

"Hey."

He was scrubbed clean, wearing a sea-green polo and a newer, darker pair of jeans.

Jeans? On a workday? His face looked oddly thin, as if he'd dropped five pounds overnight, and dark gray smudges under his eyes gave the game away: he hadn't slept. Compassion took center stage once again, but anger hadn't yet left the building.

He stepped around the table, so it was no longer between them, but didn't come any closer. He seemed to be searching painfully for something to say.

Good. Let him suffer.

Finally, he managed. "You okay?"

She glanced at Marlene, who was watching her with a huge, welcoming smile on her face. This was not the time. "Fine," she managed. "Thank you."

He'd caught the glance she threw in his mother's direction, and understood. "Good." He nodded.

He didn't get a chance to say anything more. Marlene was upon her, arms open. "Natalie! Sweetheart!" She kissed Kendra on both cheeks and stood back, smiling. Looking pleased at having successfully manipulated their evening out together. "How was your night out without me hanging around your neck like a millstone?"

Kendra couldn't help looking at Trey again, and the resulting flush was a dead giveaway. He, on the other hand, was wearing a face worthy of a poker tournament.

"That good, huh?" Marlene sparkled. She waved at the table. "Then you must be hungry. Fuel up. We've already eaten, so everything there's up for grabs."

Kendra hesitated, not just because of the awkwardness between her and Trey, but because she was pretty sure she'd stepped in on a family argument. "I'm not that hungry, really…." Lie. She was hungry enough to kill and eat a goat.

He moved forward. She was terrified he might brush against her, but he pulled out a chair in a single smooth movement and motioned for her to sit. "Come on. Sit with us. Let me pour you some coffee."

"But I'm intruding."

Marlene took care of that idea with a dismissive wave of her hand. "Oh, crud, honey child. Sit. Eat. You belong here. I'm the intruder." She gave Trey a look that could have shot a sparrow out of the sky. "As my son has wasted no time in telling me."

"Now, honestly—"

"He's had enough of me around. I don't blame him. A house-guest's welcome lasts about as long as a dead fish, I always say. When a body's welcome runs out, it's time to get going."

Trey closed his eyes, as if trying to keep a grip on his patience. "Your welcome hasn't run out."

"Cramping his style...." Marlene lifted her brows meaningfully at Kendra.

"You aren't. I love having you."

"So you say, but actions speak louder than words. He's trying to talk me into going back to his father. Can you believe that? I mean, the gall. Have a biscuit. I baked those myself. It's not that Pillsbury's stuff *he's* got in the freezer." She jerked her thumb at Trey as though buying prefab baking dough was a hangin' crime.

Kendra thought it was best to do as she was told. She buttered up a big, flaky biscuit and took a bite.

Trey struggled to keep the conversation on track. "I'm trying to get you to talk to Pops, but it's not because I don't want you here. You need to go back to him because he's your husband. You can't just get up one morning and walk out of a man's life. Not after so many years. You love him. He loves you."

"He's overprotective and boring." Marlene rolled her eyes at Kendra. "This boy's father doesn't let me do anything! We used to go dancing twice a month. We used to go to socials— and not only church socials, either, because, you know, his father's just like him. Not into all that church stuff, bless their poor souls. We used to play tennis—"

"Mom, I'm not too sure tennis is exactly what the doctor ordered for someone in your condition."

"It's not about my condition, and it's not about tennis. He's using that as an excuse. Just as you're using it as an excuse to stop me from going to see my pyramids."

"It's not an excuse. It's a legitimate reason—"

Marlene went on as if he hadn't even spoken. "No sir. It's about him plopping himself down in front of the television day in, day out, skimming them channels morning, noon and night, ever since he retired. He used to have a purpose. I used to be part of that purpose. Now my only purpose is to get him a sandwich when the game's on."

Trey looked relieved. At least Marlene was finally giving them an inkling into why she'd left. "Then let me talk to him," he volunteered. "Maybe he just needs to know that."

"I won't have you running interference between me and my husband, young man. What makes you think you can talk to your father about stuff like that? He used to wipe your butt, you know."

"Three and a half decades ago. Pops and I talk man-to-man now, in case you haven't noticed." Trey's tender, amused smile took Kendra by surprise. The stoic, expressionless face was transformed, and he became the man she'd been loving last night, if only briefly.

"Hang your britches however high you want to hang them. But keep out of this. I don't need your help. I can handle this on my own."

"You're *not* handling it on your own, or you wouldn't be here."

Marlene's jutting lower lip said she was losing. She turned to the other female for help. The only problem was, that female was still embarrassed at being dragged into a family thing. "Back me up here, Natalie, honey. It ain't right, is it? When a man who used to keep you happy in the bedroom suddenly starts having an affair with ESPN? He knows better than that, and if he cared a hoot he'd be handling his business." Then, as if anybody needed any clarification, she added, "I like my sex plenty and I like my sex good."

"Mom!"

"Oh, grow up. You know damn well we didn't find you under a cabbage patch. And don't play the age card on me, either. I'm not ready for the geriatric home." Marlene was so outraged at the implication that Kendra had to cough her laughter into a paper napkin. "Natalie, you understand, don't you? How'd you feel if my son stopped giving you a regular dose of loving?"

"Marlene!"

"Mom!"

Marlene waved her hands in wide arcs like she was directing a plane into a hangar. "Oh, right. Like butter don't melt in your mouth. Who d'you two think you're fooling? Natalie here walking in this morning, blooming like an African violet, and you—" she pointed at Trey "—looking all worn out." In spite of her irritation with her son, she was filled with mischief. "Too beat even to make it to work."

Kendra was mortified. It wasn't often a man's mother gave you a good tweaking about your activities with her son the night before.

"I'm taking the day off because I have business to attend to," Trey said briskly, bringing a decisive end to Kendra's torment. "And we weren't talking about Natalie and me, we're talking about you and Pops."

"Same principle," Marlene began.

"No, it isn't. We're dropping this conversation right now, Mom." Trey went on firmly. "But we'll be taking it up again later—after I have a talk with Pops."

"Don't you dare!"

"He's my father, and I can call him if I've a mind to."

Marlene grouched, "You're too big for a spanking, but I can still wring your ears."

"Wring away. I'll even sit so you can get at them. But I've got to do what I've got to do. And right now, I have to get out of here."

Marlene got up, still huffy. "Suit yourself. I'm going upstairs for a while. And if you aren't opposed to the inconvenience, I'll be using your phone. I need to call 'round to a few hotels and see if they have any rooms available." She gave her son the blackest of looks.

"You know you're not calling any hotels, Mom. Why don't you take it easy and watch a few movies? I'll be back early, and then we can go out. We can do whatever you like."

Marlene's only response was an eye roll and a grunt, and then she flounced out of the kitchen and up the stairs.

Trey rolled his eyes in exasperated imitation of his mother. "She's not going to call any hotels," he repeated, for Kendra's benefit and for his.

"Probably not," she agreed, for want of anything better to say.

Now they were alone. How dead was the art of conversation? They were about to find out. *You first,* she instructed silently. *Say something.*

He did talk, but there was nothing earth-shattering about his mundane question. "What're your plans for today?"

Whatever she'd been planning before, she was changing them now. She wasn't in the mood to hang around and bear the brunt of Marlene's sly, interrogatory looks. She mumbled, "I won't be staying, Trey. I've got…stuff to do." Whatever "stuff" Trey had going on, she could have, too.

Whether he took her excuse at face value or not was moot. He nodded, located his car keys and headed out. She followed, keeping several steps behind for fear of approaching the door at the same time, in case they accidentally made contact. He let her out and locked the door behind him. They regarded each other soberly on the top step, which was feeling mighty small. His expression was guarded. "Can I give you a lift?"

Be alone in a car with him? Even worse! "I'm, uh…it's okay. I sort of feel like walking."

He examined her face, looking as though he wanted to say something, but disappointingly, simply said, "Okay."

She dawdled on the step long enough to watch him get into his car, start up the engine and pull out of the drive, and then, weighed down by the burden of things said and unsaid, she stepped into the street.

Kendra's day of doing nothing was pretty much that. She wandered around De Menzes Park, feeding bread crumbs to a variety of critters. The buskers were out, so for a few dollars she listened to moody sax melodies by a skinny Goth girl, and calypso pinged out on a pair of steel pans by a freakishly tall Rastafarian in a dashiki.

She was back in her apartment by early afternoon, and spent the next few hours paying down the most critical bills from her transformation and her new life and thinking, or rather, feeling, as a range of emotions tramped through her one after the other like a marching band. First on parade was tenderness, and a need to help Trey through this time of pain. She felt privileged to have used her body to console him. She supposed that was evidence of the earth goddess hidden deep inside every woman, yearning to nurture some lost little creature. Then lust took center stage; all the altruism in the world didn't negate the fact that she'd enjoyed it. Sleeping with a man like Trey Hammond couldn't be classified as a sacrifice. She longed to feel him again.

But that wasn't going to happen. Judging by his hasty exit, he regretted their encounter with every ounce of his being. It was just his sense of decency that made him treat her with courtesy this morning. He'd been so anxious to get out of her presence, it was a wonder he hadn't slipped and tumbled down the stairs.

Which made her angry. How embarrassing it was to have a

man regret sleeping with you! Forget him, she decided. Mistake made. Lesson learned. Move on. She had an invigorating shower, blasting her best Lilith Fair-worthy, Alanis Morissette-angry, ball-bustin' CD compilation at full volume. By the time she vaulted into bed, humming a few bars of Gloria Gaynor's "I Will Survive," she was still feeling like a goddess, but a whole lot more like Kali and a lot less like Gaea.

At least she didn't have to face Trey again until morning. She'd have to go back to his house. She couldn't skulk at home forever. But she had the whole night in which to brace herself. Then the doorbell rang.

She knew at once who it was. What the hell could he want? Long after the sound of the bell had faded, she was still sitting on the bed, immobile.

The bell rang again, sounding more insistent, more urgent, even though it had just one tone. Feeling considerably less goddess-like, she got out of bed, went over, and unlocked the door without even looking through the peephole. He was wearing the same clothes as this morning, much the worse for wear—as if he'd spent the day tramping the streets or sleeping in his car. The polo was rumpled, and had ridden up out of the waistband of his jeans. His eyes were shadowed with lilac half-moons, and the dark pupils looked as though someone had plucked two celestial bodies clean out of the starry night, leaving a vast emptiness.

"Trey…" She stood aside, offering wide access to her apartment. When he didn't move, she beckoned him. "Come in."

He stepped inside, as oblivious to his surroundings, this time, as he had been curious the night before. She locked the door behind him, noticing her hands were shaking. He'd decided to reprise his mantle of silence once more, but oddly enough, it didn't irritate her. His harrowed face told her more than she needed to hear. She held her arms out to him. They kissed, as long as they had the night before, and as hungrily.

Then they proceeded to the corner dominated by her bed and stripped down, each removing his or her own clothes, without embarrassment, but without sensuality, either.

But this time things were different. Better. No longer happy just to take what she offered, he was more focused on giving. And giving, and giving. His hands roamed her body, seeking and touching. Coaxing and teasing.

He returned her favor of last night, delving between her legs and licking her quivering, plum-dark wetness until spasms shook her to her toes. His fingers joined in, slipping deep inside her, twisting until they found the right spot. Then he curled them forward as though calling her, insistently beckoning her over the cliff. She came willingly.

Her thighs were so tightly clenched around his wrist that he had to pry them apart to get his hand back. She was relieved that he'd stopped; she couldn't stand another moment of such intensity. But her respite was only momentary. In one deft move, he had her flat on her tummy, a pillow jammed under her pelvis to bring her to just the right angle. Then he swooped down and spread himself out upon her.

Last night had been the dress rehearsal; tonight was the command performance. This time, there was nothing for him to apologize for. He was all muscle, bone and driving intensity. And she loved it.

Oh, but the silence. She didn't expect him to kick up a racket or whisper a stream of dirty talk, but the impenetrable silence was eerie. It was as though she was making love to an astral projection of the man rather than the man himself. And again, there was this haunting—the sensation that the two of them were not alone in her bed. It was all she could do not to call, tentatively, into the night, "Ashia…?"

When he rolled over beside her, she pressed against his damp, quiet body, so she could feel his breathing slow once again. She had to break the silence. Not to do so would have driven her mad. And what better subject to address than the one that was eating away at him like acid? Much as he had done last night, she reached down and touched the wedding band on his ring finger. It was as warm as human flesh. "She wouldn't hold it against you, Trey. She'd understand."

He turned his head toward her. "I know."

"So don't beat yourself up."

"Takes some getting used to."

"What?"

"The feel of another woman. The *idea* of another woman. I've been faithful to Ashia since the night we met."

"That's an awful long time."

"It is." He drew his brows together, thinking hard. "I didn't expect that it would be like this."

"Like what?" She waited on tenterhooks for an answer.

His assessment fell like a bomb. "Safe."

Safe? How odd. Better than "lousy", but still odd. "What's that mean?" She wasn't sure if her pride should be injured or not.

He was still addressing the ceiling rather than her. "I thought I'd be sick with shame. In a way, the reason I've stayed away from women and…this…isn't all about Ashia and how I feel about her. Part of it was that I was sure I'd hate myself."

"Do you?"

"No."

"Good, because you have no reason to."

"I know that. Intellectually. But the intellect and the emotions don't usually keep each other company."

"What do your emotions say?" The word "tenterhooks" was becoming quite literal; anxiety and anticipation dug into her flesh as she waited for him to answer.

He thought for way too long for any good to come of whatever he would say next. She considered ending the conversation with a huffy "forget it," and rolling over onto her side, letting her bare back tell him how she felt about that, but this was way too important for her to spoil it through pique.

It was worth the wait. He shifted so he could look at her. "They're saying a whole lot of odd things. Stuff I wasn't expecting."

"Good stuff?" Why was she hoping so hard?

"Wonderful stuff."

Then they were kissing again, with more romance than passion. He touched her in a way that told her he was trying to caress her mind as well as her body, but her body wasn't jealous. She was ready to say "the hell with conversation, let our bodies do the talking," but he stopped and lifted his head.

Come on, Kendra, she chided herself for her disappointment, when he's silent, you want him to say something; when he's talking, you want him to shut up. She commanded her body to stop complaining and listen.

"There's something I have to tell you. Something you need to know if this is ever to…go anywhere."

Where'd he want to take this? "I'm listening."

"It's about that ship in the bottle. The one you…the one I flipped out over when you touched it. You need to understand what happened to Ashia, and why I—"

She was pleased that he was willing to share something so intimate with her, but to spare him the pain of recounting the story, she interrupted. "You don't have to. Don't hurt yourself telling it. I know. Your mom told me." As she said it, she half-cringed, wondering if he'd be mad at her for snooping.

Instead, he smiled. "Trust Marlene to get to you first."

In case he deflected his ire at his mother instead, she hastened to tell him, "She was only trying to help. She wanted to make sure things were going okay between you and me. You and Natalie, I mean."

"She doesn't think things are okay between me and… Natalie?"

"Not really. She's been trying to help me understand why you're not as, uh, demonstrative as a man in love should be. In case I'm, uh, feeling underappreciated." She couldn't hold back an abashed grin.

"Well, she's not dumb. I guess if you looked hard enough, you could tell that we weren't as…intimate as we were trying to have her believe."

"Until this morning."

He laughed softly. "Until this morning."

The memory of getting made by Marlene practically before she even entered Trey's house made Kendra heat up. "And she sure was tickled."

He shook his head in amusement. "Sure was. She's probably convinced herself it was all her idea. And you know by now, what Marlene wants, Marlene gets. There's no force in the universe more powerful than a woman with grandbabies on her agenda."

Maybe it was due to the long-lasting effects of good sex, or maybe she was just dopey from lack of sleep, but that made Kendra smile. Kids. With Trey. For a way-too-long minute there, she found herself wondering if his and "Natalie's" children would have gray eyes. But she made sure the thought perished. Instead, she asked, "What're you going to do about that?"

"About the grandbabies?"

She punched him on the bicep, hard. "About your mother and this whole Natalie escapade. Don't you think it's cruel, getting her hopes up?"

He rubbed his arm thoughtfully. "Maybe it is, although I swear, I was trying to be kind." He sighed. "I guess I'll have to tell her soon. I just need to think of the best way. But for the time being…"

"The show must go on." She made a face.

"You still okay with that?"

"I still don't like it, but I'm doing all right."

"Thank you again." He kissed her lightly on the brow.

She could have said "no problem," but that wouldn't have been accurate, so she indicated the two of them, still wrapped around each other, with a twirl of her finger, and said, "This changes things a little."

"Yes, it does."

What things were changed, and how exactly they'd changed, she wasn't sure she wanted to analyze. Instead, she ventured to reach out and stroke his body, up and down the length of his torso and up to his face, to trace his hairline with her fingertip. He closed his eyes and let her stroke his jaw. "It's been a long time since I've felt like a whole man."

"You feel like a whole man to me," she said saucily.

He actually laughed, and the effect was amazing. Not something she was used to, and especially not something she was used to making him do. Seriously, she said "I know things have been hard, but you've got every reason to feel good about yourself. You've done well, especially for someone so young. You've got your own business and your own home. Ashia would've been proud of you. You just need to ground yourself again. Lighten up. Embrace life." She wanted to add, "Embrace me."

"Lighten up," he echoed thoughtfully. "You don't how hard I've tried. How far I've come. What you see, the man you know, is only half of who I was, but I've come a long way from what I'd turned into. There was a time even my own mother couldn't look at me without crying."

"Really?" She tried not to sound too eager for the insight into himself he was offering, but he wasn't often in the mood for intimate sharing. She felt like she'd been handed a pass into an exclusive club. A temporary pass, but a pass all the same.

"Really. For a whole year after the accident, I didn't cut my hair or shave. I only showered when the dogs couldn't stand to be around me any more. I lost forty pounds. I got to work later and later and eventually gave up going in at all. My bosses were understanding at first, but after a while…." He shrugged.

"Business is business."

"I lost my job. Then my car, then my home. I had to move back in with my folks. And I didn't care. I bummed around, cursed God and stared at the walls."

She squinted at him, trying to imagine him with dirty baby dreads and an unshaven chin. "How'd you get over that? What happened?"

"My father happened. My mother had been pleading with me for months to get it together. She prayed, begged and bullied, but I tuned her out. Then one day my Pops got fed up with me moping around, cracked me one on the jaw and kicked me to the curb. Literally. He gave me twenty dollars and told me if I wanted to be a bum I could feel free, just don't do it on his turf."

"Good."

"I didn't feel that way at the time. The only thing that kept me from cracking him one right back—or trying to, he's bigger than I am—was the last shred of self-respect I had left. I didn't want to stoop as low as hitting my elder."

Kendra didn't think that Trey would have gone that far even in the worst of circumstances. "So what'd you do?"

"I spent the night on the sidewalk, thinking. In the morning I walked down to the barbershop and spent that twenty on a haircut and a shave. Then I went back home, knocked on the door and gave my father a hug. We drank a few beers and both cried like babies. Then we sat down and hashed out a plan to save my life."

"It was a good plan, whatever it was," she complimented him. "Look at you now."

"Good. Slow and painstaking, but good. I found a job quickly, thank God. I saved money, built back up my credit, and looked around for a business I could invest in that'd let me be everything I wanted to be—self-sufficient, dependable, and trustworthy."

"And you found Shel's place."

"Yep. It was a stretch, financially, and even so, my father had to pump a considerable amount of his and Mom's retirement fund into the deal, but I made it. I'm in hock up to my eyeballs, and I don't own anything free and clear, except for the food in my cupboard and the shirt on my back—"

"You aren't wearing a shirt," she reminded him, circling his nipple with the edge of her fingernail.

He flinched, and gave in to an erotic shudder, but didn't shy away. He tried to continue his point. "I'm going to make sure I don't let my folks down."

"You won't. You're a good man, and you're smart enough and passionate enough about your business to make it work. Your dad's done a terrific job with you."

"He's a great guy. That's why this whole tomfoolery with Mom leaving him has got to stop. She has a way of flying off the deep end, saying and doing stuff she shouldn't, and then not being able to back down and admit she's made a mistake. Deep down, she's longing to go back to Pops, she's just afraid to admit she was wrong. They're right for each other, and I plan to show her that."

"How?"

He smiled mysteriously. "I've got a few plans I'll be setting in motion." Then he reached for her. "But not tonight."

Chapter 10

Lazarus

Kendra woke to find that the gorgeous man who'd worn her out well into the early hours was now sleeping soundly at her side, completely naked, his back to her. And what a view! Even in rest, the musculature of his powerful back was like that of a matador—a triangle formed by broad shoulders, sloping lats, and a sudden narrowing at his waist. Below, there were faint red scratches on his toned, perfect backside that hadn't been there when he'd arrived. Note to self: trim nails. She sat up and cocked her head to one side, the better to admire him. He was as golden as the rays of sunlight that streaked in through the half-open blinds and cut broad, bright stripes across the rumpled sheets.

But admiration was just the half of it. There was also relief; he hadn't snuck away during the night. That possibility had been her last thought before she faded into sleep in his arms. Maybe his postcoital disappearing trick, like his muteness, would prove to be a one-night-only performance. She hoped so. Of course, that was assuming there'd be more nights together for her and Trey, and maybe that meant she was getting a little bit ahead of herself. Two nights in bed with a man didn't mean a relationship.

She leaned closer. He smelled warm and manly—and familiar, somehow. Then she realized that the scent she was recognizing was her own, steeped into his skin during their heated encounters. She looked down at him, watching his breathing, marveling at how strong her feelings for him had become. Would he mind if she touched him right now, intimately, lovingly, even though they weren't making love?

Without warning, he flipped onto his back and opened his eyes. For a brief moment he looked surprised, maybe even a little confused; but as memory dawned, his confusion didn't morph into dismay. So far, so good. He raised himself onto one elbow and pressed a kiss onto her bare shoulder. "Good morning."

"Good morning." She gave in to her impulse, consequences be damned, and touched him gently, tracing the shape of his brow with her fingertip, even though a little thing like a touch could betray her feelings. "How you doing?"

He frowned as though she'd thrown out a stumper on *Who Wants to Be a Millionaire:* Are you a) still horny, b) hungry enough to eat deep-fried hippo, c) bitterly regretful or d) searching for an excuse to find yourself anywhere but here? He sat up and—oh, God, he's glorious naked. She shook her head. Focus, Kendra, for Pete's sake. The man's saying something.

"I feel…" He rubbed his head as though he'd been whacked from behind. "I feel like…Lazarus."

She hadn't seen that coming. "Lazarus?" Maybe he was delirious. Had he had dinner last night, before coming over?

Maybe his blood sugar was low. Did she have any hard candy on the bedside table?

"Yes." He looked surprised to hear himself say it. "I feel like I've just woken up from a long, cold sleep, and walked out of my own tomb." When his eyes held hers, she found it impossible to look away. "And you did that to me."

You did that. The implications were staggering. Given all he'd said to her about the hell he'd been through, to think that somehow, by being there for him, with him, she'd helped him stumble out of the darkness and into the light...*well!*

He was as bowled over as she was; but whereas she was smiling in bemused pleasure, he still wore a puzzled frown. "How'd that happen?"

Was this it, then? The part where he trundled out the tired old "it's not you, it's me" speech, got dressed, and beat it? Kendra's smile left her. She drew in her lip and bit down on it hard to keep it from trembling. She folded her arms over her breasts, feeling more naked than naked. *Go ahead then,* she signaled silently. *Let's get it over with.*

He didn't get the message. Without saying anything more, he got up and found his way to her bathroom, stumbling about like a groggy bear. That was all? He wasn't going to say any more? She watched him go, stunned, feeling like a victim of *conversationus interruptus.* She rose, too, unsure of what to do now. What was the etiquette when you woke up with a man in your bed? Breakfast—that was it. Maybe he'd say what he had to say better on a full belly. "Hungry?" She had to raise her voice to be heard over the sound of rushing water.

"Starving, but I really have to be going," he yelled back.

Sure you do. Against her better judgment, she hovered outside the bathroom door. She couldn't resist the urge to go in and talk to him—but he was in the bathroom. He deserved his privacy. And he'd be naked. But what the heck, it was her bathroom, and it wasn't like they'd been playing tiddledywinks all night. She'd seen him as naked as he could get. She stepped in.

He was wet and golden and amazing, skin glowing as he scrubbed it down under the steaming flow. She was sidetracked for a moment, watching him. Back turned to her, he bent over to soap his feet….oh, my. Whoever said that men were more easily aroused by visual stimuli didn't know what they were talking about. Could any woman ever get tired of such a sight? Then she remembered her purpose for entering. "You're sure I can't offer you anything? Coffee?"

He turned to her, water dripping off his eyelashes and down his lips. "I'd love to, honey, but time's against me."

"Late for work?" Lord, let it be as simple as that.

"Very. But I'm going to be even later. I've got an errand to run."

"Got to make sure your Mom's okay?"

He was shampooing his hair, all bubbles and suds. "I'm sure Mom's fine. I'll give her a call to let her know I'm alive. But by now she's probably turned my extra curtains into placemats and alphabetized my CD collection, so I'm not too worried about her. I'm in a rush because I have to go to the airport."

"You traveling?" She tried not to let him hear her disappointment. She was missing him already, and there was only four feet of air between them.

"Nope. Gotta pick someone up." Then he made her day. "Wanna come?"

"Really?"

"Sure. I'd love your company."

She couldn't stop the grin from spreading. "I'd like that."

He peered at his watch through the cloud of steam. "Well, we've got about, oh, I'd say eight minutes to ride out of here if we want to be on time. That means we'd better conserve time *and* water. Hop in."

He was inviting her to shower with him? That sent her pleasure receptors popping like a string of firecrackers set off by pranksters in a high school hallway. He must have read the devilry on her face, because he imposed a caveat. "Just don't touch me, Forrest, because if I get caught up in you again, my Pops is taking a taxi home."

Ah, so his dad was coming. Trey was planning on doing some matchmaking—or rematchmaking. "Staring, good. Touching, bad. Check." She didn't have anything to take off, so she sidled gingerly into the small shower stall, taking his warning seriously and not brushing up against him, as that delightful prospect would have kicked off a whole 'nother ball game—no pun intended.

Rushworth International Airport was in chaos. People moved in a blur. Some dragged suitcases behind them, like oversized dogs at a kennel show. Some hugged each other, crying tears of hello or farewell. Some hawked trinkets, others hawked salvation, both keeping on eye out for the airport cops. Kendra wasn't able to focus on much of that, though. Something else was weighing on her mind.

Apart from being irrationally nervous at the prospect of meeting Trey's father, there was the whole Natalie thing. He'd lied to his mother, but was Hammond Senior in on the scam, or had Trey duped him, too? If so, Trey would expect her to lie to his father. The rules of the Natalie game kept changing on her. She wasn't sure she liked it.

Trey moved purposefully upstream, glancing back to make sure she was still with him. He caught sight of her expression. "Don't be afraid. My Pops is the coolest man alive."

"I'm not afraid. I'm…" She stopped, resolutely, and he had no choice but to stop, too, or yank her arm out of her shoulder. "You want me to be Natalie for your father, too, don't you."

He nodded, slowly. "I know this isn't easy for you. But what were you expecting? I never attempted to sell him on the Natalie story, but Mom's been going on and on about her for months in his presence."

"But—"

"But what? I could tell him the truth, but he doesn't deserve to have any more stuff on his mind right now. The poor guy flew halfway up the coast to try to get his wife back. Second, if I come clean with him, I'd have to ask him to keep up with the charade for Mom's sake, and that's not fair. So this seems like the only viable option."

He was making sense, but that didn't make her feel any better. He read her doubt and looked genuinely contrite. "I'm sorry. I know this wasn't part of the deal, but please…" He placed both hands on her shoulders. "Kendra, sweetheart, I need you to do this for me."

Well, when he put it that way… She pushed her foreboding to the back of her mind and tried to smile. "It's okay. I think I can handle it."

He pressed a kiss to her lips. "I know you can." Then he added fervently, "I owe you one." Then her hand was in his and they were hurrying along again.

Spotting Trey's father in a crowd was a breeze. They just had to look above the heads of the tallest people in the room and there he was. Trey raised his arm in welcome. The older man smiled and waved back. The crowd made it difficult to get through, which gave Kendra time to examine him. He was a well-built, handsome man, and his eyes, a paler version of Trey's, were framed by thin glasses. His sandy hair was longer than Trey's and almost as wavy, shot through with silver. He had Trey's angular face and wide mouth. The same long nose. The same easy posture and athletic walk. And Trey hadn't been kidding, his father was bigger than he was, and powerfully built, though he had to be close to sixty.

Kendra stepped discreetly aside as the two men hugged warmly and exchanged greetings. Then Trey's eyes searched her out, as if he were anxious to bring her into their circle. He held out his hand to her. "Come meet my father."

She stepped obediently forward, holding out her hand. "Hi."

The older man didn't take her hand, but instead put his arms around her and hugged her as warmly as he had his son. "You must be Natalie. It's so good to meet you. My wife talks so much about you." He glanced at his son. "Or she did, back when she was speaking to me." His face creased briefly, but his warm smile came quickly again. "I'm Robert."

"Nice to meet you, Robert."

Trey stepped in. "Don't worry about this whole thing with Mom, Pops. We're going to get our heads together and get her to come around."

Robert laughed ruefully. "Never thought I'd be needing my son to help save my marriage."

"Oh, *you'll* be doing the saving. I'm just greasing the wheels a little." With that assurance, he guided them out of the fray, back into the sunshine. They found their car without too much trouble. Robert tossed his things in the trunk and, as Trey held the front passenger door open, said to Kendra. "In you go, young lady."

She protested. "You haven't seen your son in months. You should be the one sitting up front with him."

"I can see him fine from the backseat. You two probably can't stand to be more'n a couple of inches apart for ten minutes, so hop in."

Trey was egging her in with a sideways toss of the head, so she quelled her protests and slid in as Robert installed himself behind her.

"I know she's pretty, son, but you try to keep both hands on the steering wheel, okay?" Robert couldn't resist cracking. "Even though your mother'll probably rip me apart later anyway, I'd at least like to turn up at your place in one piece."

"I can steer with my knees if I have to, you know."

"Don't even think about it. Matter of fact, why'n't you two lovebirds just climb on into the back seat and let me drive?" Robert asked, and then mischievously informed Kendra, "I did a whole lot of that from the time he was about fourteen, you know. Wanting to impress his girlfriends by picking them up in a car, but too young to drive. Oh, yeah, I spent my share of Saturday nights outside pizza joints, waiting on him and his dates."

"And I'll be forever grateful, Pops. I know it wasn't easy, giving up your weekends."

"Don't worry, I got a lot of reading done. Besides, when y'all have kids of your own, you'll know what it's like. Watching you get frazzled will be payback enough for me." His laugh was exactly like Trey's.

Kids? They sure had high expectations. She glanced involuntarily at Trey. His eyes were on her. She turned and looked out the window, wondering if he was going to respond.

He didn't, at least not on *that* subject. Kendra settled down for the journey, happy to keep silent and allow the men to reminisce, talk about Trey's progress with his business, and swap sports stories. As they entered the city, Trey suggested, "Want to stop to get something to eat before you face the Dragon Lady, Pops?"

"I hope you don't call her that to her face."

"I'm not stupid. I'm kind of partial to my kneecaps, thanks. So, you hungry?"

Please, please, please be hungry, Kendra pleaded silently. She was on her way to a hypoglycemic meltdown. Food! Food! Food!

Robert thought for a while, but said, "Uh, sounds good, but the sooner I get there, the less nervous I'll be. Don't think I'd even be able to swallow."

I could, Kendra thought, I could swallow a whole lot. But she maintained a polite silence.

"Wouldn't mind stopping at your flower shop, though," he added.

"*My* flower shop?"

"Wherever it is you go to buy your pretty little lady here some flowers."

Trey was abashed. "Well, actually…"

Robert groaned and leaned forward to address Kendra. "Don't tell me my son's never bought you flowers?"

Cover for him? Or let him swing in the wind? She was leaning toward the letting-him-swing option, but Trey fessed up. "I've got to admit, Pops, I've been a little lax in that department."

Robert snorted. "That makes you more like your dumb old man than you think. It's little oversights like that that's got me in this lonely boat without your mother. A hundred careless little mistakes, not the one or two big blunders that I might have made. I used to bring her flowers—for no reason. All the time."

"I remember," Trey said indulgently.

Robert went on dolefully. "I slowed down. Then I stopped. I used to turn up in the middle of the afternoon with a bottle of wine under my arm and a stupid grin on my face. I stopped doing that, too." He gave a lonely sigh. "And so, here I am, crawling back, hoping to convince her not to choose stinky camels and dusty old mummified pharaohs over me."

Kendra felt sorry for him. She wished she knew him well enough to reach back and pat him on the hand. Robert leaned forward again. "Let me tell you something, Trey. Whatever you do with your relationship, you got to keep it fresh. You got to do whatever you can, even if it means not working so hard, although I know you have a new business to run. Don't let it take *all* of your time."

"I understand."

"You'd better. It doesn't take a cataclysm to kill love. You don't need an affair or a betrayal or a huge fight to break a person's heart. All it takes is a little selfishness, a little overfamiliarity and a little neglect."

Kendra could feel Trey's eyes on her. She could feel them until her skin burned, but she wouldn't, couldn't, flat-out refused to, turn to meet his gaze.

"I hear you, Pops." Out of the corner of her eye she could see Trey was smiling. "Natalie?"

It was several seconds before she realized he was calling her. "Trey?"

"Could you direct these two out-of-towners to a flower shop?"

"There's a really nice one on Independence," she suggested. Then she added pointedly, "Right next to the Starbucks store."

"On our way."

Kendra waited quietly while the two Hammond men poked around in the flower shop, talking over the comparative qualities of this bloom over that with the attendant. Robert liked lavish bunches, while Trey favored long-stalked flowers with clean lines and crisp, fresh colors. In spite of their indecision and arguments, they never consulted her, determined to make their choice without feminine input.

The men came toward her with their arms full, both grinning proudly, as though they'd nurtured and grown the flowers from seedlings. Robert held a huge bouquet of milk-white roses, lilies and orchids, made all the more stunning by the brilliant yellow sunflowers snuggled between them. "Marlene carried white and yellow flowers on our wedding day," he explained. "Orchids in her hair. A big, puffy, seventies Afro with orchids stuck in it all over. She was beautiful."

"Your flowers are gorgeous, Robert. She'll love them."

"There," Trey encouraged. "A woman's point of view. You'll be fine."

"Okay," Robert said, but he didn't sound any less nervous.

Trey was holding a much smaller, less elaborate offering: a dozen tulips, ranging in shades of pink, from hothouse fuchsia to baby's blush. They were wrapped in a sheet of crackling white tissue and tied together with a satin ribbon as green as their stems. He held them out to her. "These are for you." He was smiling like a Christmas elf.

"Attaboy," Robert encouraged.

Kendra took them, unable to mouth her thanks. She cradled them against her heart, trying to remind herself that this was all part of the charade. All to impress Trey's father, convince him that this thing he felt for "Natalie" was real. But even though she knew the truth, she couldn't stop herself from bringing them to her lips, feeling the softness of the petals. The combined fragility and strength of the petals reminded her of how his most delicate skin had felt against her lips the night before. She shivered.

She felt Trey's hand at her elbow as he guided her outside. Robert was close on their heels, hugging his horticultural monster securely in both arms.

"One more thing," Trey said, and disappeared into the Starbucks next door. Robert lifted his brows at her, but she shrugged. Trey returned holding a sandwich and a steaming cup of coffee. "French vanilla okay?"

She was puzzled. "What?"

He grinned. "I wouldn't want you tripping on me when your blood sugar bottoms." He handed over the goods. "You can eat in the car."

Bless you, she thought, and sniffed the engaging aromas of foamy milk, hot coffee, roast turkey and mustard. *Seems you know what I want both in and out of bed.* She was overwhelmed by his thoughtfulness. It was almost as if he were courting her for real.

Chapter 11

Revelation

It didn't take them long to realize Marlene wasn't inside the house. Trey walked through, calling for her, but the only sound that came back was one of her old church choir recordings playing in the bedroom upstairs. The back door was open. Kendra and Robert followed Trey to find Marlene at the far end of the garden, bent forward, fiddling with the dilapidated child's seesaw. She heard them coming but didn't turn around.

"Trey, when're you going to get this poor old seesaw fixed? All it needs is a few bolts and a lick of paint."

"Who's going to ride on it, Mom?"

"Never mind who. It's a fine seesaw, and it'd be a crying shame if you just leave it here in your backyard, lying on its side like a sick old dog."

Trey was patient but firm. "I've got enough stuff to do with this house to last me a long time, so a seesaw in a house without children isn't one of my priorities."

"You ask me, you got your priorities on backwards." Marlene tugged on the contraption, and a chunk of it fell away. She sucked her teeth in exasperation. "You should *make* it a priority. You're thirty-five. What you waiting on? You want to start having kids when you're too old to give them horsie rides? Right, Natalie? As for you, you're young *now,* but before you know it, you're looking for a doctor to shoot you up full of fertility drugs. Wind up with quints or something, when you could'a had 'em one by one, like God intended."

Kendra stood there, hugging her tulips to her chest, afraid to speak. Robert's voice rumbled from behind her shoulder. "Give the kids a break, Marlene. They aren't even engaged yet, and here you are, talking about seesaws and children."

Marlene spun around so fast she almost fell over. "Robert!" For a minute, she wasn't able to disguise the surprised delight on her face, but then she remembered there was a war on. She covered up her pleasure with a scowl. "What're you doing here?"

Robert had a brave smile pasted on, but the tension was revealed in the deep lines in the corners of his eyes. "I'm looking for my wife. Have you seen her?"

"Bet you think that's funny."

"Just trying to put back that smile that was there seven seconds ago. What happened to it?"

Marlene shoved her fists into the pockets of her print dress. The bumps looked like tennis balls. "I remembered I'm mad at you."

"If you need to remember, maybe you're not all that mad." He held out the armload of flowers. "I brought you these."

Kendra felt sorry for him. Judging from the expression on Marlene's face, getting that smile back was going to be an uphill battle. The fists in Marlene's pockets bumped against her thighs. "Why? What you bring me those for?"

"Because I love you and I want you to have them. They

remind me of our wedding day." His warm memories of the day were alive in his eyes.

Marlene faltered, then her lips twisted. "Huh. A likely story." She turned to Trey, who was standing by, watching the exchange with his arms folded, a worried frown on his face. "You put him up to this?"

"The flowers? No," he answered mildly.

"You know that's not what I meant. You tell him I was here?"

"Course I did. He was worried about you."

"Well, you had no right." The tennis ball in her left pocket transformed itself back into a hand, poking in the direction of Trey's chest. *"No right."*

Trey's tone was as mild and as respectful as before, but every bit as firm. "I've got every right to talk to my father."

She snorted. "You tell him to come over here?"

"No, that was his decision, too."

Marlene cocked her head to one side. Her eyes were accusing slits. "But you sent him a ticket."

Kendra watched Trey's heavy shoulders lift and fall. "I own travel agencies. Plane tickets litter the ground like leaves."

Marlene's finger was a dart aimed at Trey's heart. "Don't get smart with me, young man. Think you can sass me just 'cause you got a little hair on your chest? Wish I could still send you to your room."

That made Trey smile, even though he knew that that was like chumming the water in a shark pool. "You're occupying that particular room at the moment, if I recall."

Marlene's dark brown eyes swiveled upward, and she addressed the heavens in the voice of a martyr. "See? I knew he was tired of me. I told you, didn't I, Lord? Didn't have to go this far, though. Wanted me out of his room, all he had to do was say. Me cramping his style and all that." She shot a meaningful look at Kendra.

Kendra wondered if the God Marlene was berating could

help her disappear. "Maybe I should…" She and her flowers began inching sideways, toward the house. "…find a vase for these. Or something." Maybe, by some miracle, there'd be a hole in the living room, and she could go bury herself in it.

The Finger of Doom jerked away from Trey's chest, and Kendra was in its sights. "You stay right there. You need to know the kind of family you're getting into—"

It was Trey's turn to interrupt. "Mom, Natalie and I've only known each other for…" He hesitated. "For a little while. Don't get beyond yourself."

"Talk about getting beyond yourself." Marlene rounded on her husband again. She still hadn't taken the flowers. "I'm not the only one. What makes you think you can walk in here with a bunch of flowers and expect me to fall all over you?"

Robert was still holding the outrageous bouquet before him, but less as an offering and more like a shield. "It's a start."

The pain and confusion on Robert's face were enough to prompt Trey to step in and play peacemaker. "Why don't we all go inside and have a drink?"

"At this hour? It's not even halfway to lunchtime. I never taught you it was okay to drink before noon."

"No, you didn't, but I was thinking we could all do with something to soothe our nerves."

"Who's getting on your nerves? Me? So I'm driving you to drink now?" Marlene seemed determined to turn even the most innocent remark into an invitation to do battle.

And to Kendra's surprise, Robert took up the challenge. "You'd drive any man to drink, give you enough time." The hand holding the flowers dropped to his side, pointing downward like a sword.

"If you came all the way over here to insult me, you could have stayed home," Marlene retorted, gleeful at having struck a nerve.

Trey and Kendra exchanged glances. "Pops, that's not helping."

Kendra decided that standing there like an idiot wasn't going to solve anything. She took the flowers from Robert and left, barely able to see past both bunches. Feeling like she was fleeing the storming of the beach at Normandy.

Inside, she took a good long time finding something to put the flowers in. As much as she loved Marlene, she wasn't about to stand around and watch her mow down the two men, especially not when the chances of her being hit by shrapnel were high. She considered making herself one of the drinks Trey had mentioned—and a stiff one at that. Instead, she made coffee, since her earlier one was now a distant memory.

A clatter in the doorway announced the arrival of the troops, and it didn't look as though any treaties had been drawn up. Trey was speaking. "All I'm saying, Mom, is you should give it a try. You haven't got anything to lose."

"I've got Giza, Egypt, to lose. That's where I'm going. And with your aunt Amelia, not with…" She threw her husband a hard look. "…anybody else."

"Mom, I don't think it's safe for you to travel that far in your condition. Even for a fit person, jaunting around the deserts of North Africa isn't the easiest holiday in the world. Think about your health."

Marlene looked uncertain. For once, she didn't have a snappy response handy.

Spotting a crack in her resistance, Trey hammered in the wedge. "You can go later in the year if your doctor says it's okay. I'll pay for the whole thing." He glanced at his father. "You can go to Egypt with anyone you choose. But not right now. All I'm asking is that you take this little trip with Pops, just a week. Talk over what you've got on your mind."

Robert chimed in. "I wouldn't have come all the way over here if I wasn't willing to listen, Marlene. Trey's right. A cruise'd do us some good. It'd give us time to talk."

She looked doubtful, but she was listening. "I don't know…Alaska sounds mighty cold."

"It's spring, Mom. It's almost as warm there as it is here." He added, knowing her penchant for frugality, "And it's free. That new tour operator I was considering offered me two all-expenses paid tickets so I could try it out for myself. You can give me a full report when you get back. Taste everything, try out all the amenities, get your hair done, have a massage. If you give it the thumbs-up, I'll take on their service." Trey pressed harder. "Do it for me."

Marlene wavered. "Would it really help you out?"

"Tremendously. I'm swamped at the office. I've been taking way too much time off to deal with house matters. There's no way I could go now, and I'd hate to miss out on a package that could be a big money maker for Wanderlust."

"And it's free?"

"Absolutely. First class, too. On one of the upper decks. You'd have a great view. And I hear sometimes the whales escort the ship along the way."

"I like whales," Marlene murmured.

"I know you do."

Robert knew what was good for him. He stayed quiet while Marlene frowned thoughtfully down at her feet.

Then, like a delayed reaction, it clicked. Kendra realized the package Trey was offering his parents was the same one she'd been researching while she worked at Wanderlust. Idiotically, she felt a ray of pride. It meant, at least, that he trusted her business judgment. She added her own encouragement. "You'll love it, Marlene. I've checked these people out myself, and I can promise you you'll have a wonderful time."

"Think so?"

"I know so," she encouraged, and added slyly, "it's very romantic."

Robert's eyebrows lifted. "You checked them out?" He looked from her to Trey and back again. "Were you two planning on… I mean, we're not depriving you of a trip you were planning to take for yourselves, are we?"

She hastened to assure them, "Oh, no, not at all. I did a professional analysis of them a few weeks ago…." She trailed off, knowing she'd said too much.

Robert looked puzzled. "You did a…?"

Marlene grudgingly informed her husband, "Natalie's in the tour business, too."

"Ah." A look of understanding. "You work for our son?"

Not that again!

Trey stepped in. "Not exactly, Dad. Kendra's between jobs right now, but she'll be back on the market in a week or so. Maybe even sooner."

The significance of that last remark was lost on the couple, but not on Kendra. Once her little acting gig was over, she was out of there. She knew he was looking at her, but she couldn't return the glance.

Robert brightened. "Well, maybe you could—"

Trey didn't even let him air the thought. "We both think that'd be a bad idea."

"Why?"

"Too complicated," Trey said firmly.

"Too complicated," Kendra said weakly.

"Oh." Robert didn't seem convinced.

Very, very complicated. As if from a distance, she could hear the others talking about the trip. From the snippets of conversation that she could catch through her haze, she could tell Marlene was coming around. But she couldn't focus. A sudden revelation had entered her mind like a bee flying in through her ear, and was buzzing around inside her skull. The deal she had with Trey was that she'd do the Natalie thing for two weeks…or until Marlene left. The tour began in three days.

When she no longer had a reason to be with Trey, what would happen? Would she see him again? She thought about last night, how different it had been from the night before. How real it had felt—at least to her. Then his words of this morning came back to her. He'd told her she'd performed a miracle, waking him up like Lazarus. He'd told her she made him feel safe.

He'd made her feel things, too. Things she wasn't used to. Fully accepted for the body she had now and the one she'd had then. He'd seen that awful photo of her on the fridge door, but it hadn't turned him off.

He'd made her feel stronger than she'd ever felt before, because in his weakness he'd allowed her, needed her, to be the strong one. He'd made her revel in her womanliness, because that was where he'd found his comfort. He'd made her feel loved.

No, that wasn't right. Trey didn't love her. That was an illusion, a mirage conjured up by her desperate subconscious, urgently seeking justification for her own feelings. She needed to believe that she was loved in order to be comfortable with the idea of being in love.

What?

No.

Her belly was a roller coaster. Love. That was *so* not on. That was crazy. Her blood sugar had dropped a little too low, was all; she'd waited too long to have that coffee and sandwich. It'd all even out any minute now, and then she'd be okay.

But as much as she wanted to, even she wasn't buying that laughable argument. She could deny it, talk herself out of it, dispute it all she wanted, but that didn't make the truth go away. She was in love with Trey Hammond.

Chapter 12

Fessing Up

No, no, no, no, no. Not right. Not true. Kendra put her hand to her head, feeling woozy as panic and incredulity swamped her. The hardwood kitchen floor she'd put so much elbow grease into had turned to liquid. It advanced and receded in waves. She put a hand out to steady herself. The floor advanced again, but this time it didn't recede.

"Kendra!"

She heard the thumping of Trey's feet and then felt his arms supporting her. He held her with one arm, awkwardly, reaching for a kitchen chair with the other. He pressed her into it. "You okay?" His face was close as he peered anxiously at her. Too close. She felt cornered. Trapped.

"I'm fine," she lied. Breathe in, breathe out.

"You still hungry? Can I get you something to eat?"

"No, I'm fine," she insisted. "Just a little dizzy. I don't know what happened. One minute I was standing there, next thing I know, I'm hitting the ground…."

"Oh, my God, she's pregnant!" Marlene slapped her hands over her mouth to keep the grin in.

Trey turned his head in his mother's direction, denying sharply, "She is not—" He stopped, looked at Kendra again, and asked a silent question.

If she hadn't been so shaken up, she'd have been insulted at the implication contained in the look. "I'm not pregnant, Trey." *And for the love of God,* she wanted to add, *please stop touching me. I can't stand it anymore.*

He was persistent. "Then what…?"

"I'm a little woozy. It's nothing. Tired, I guess. It'll pass." She struggled weakly against him, but he didn't relinquish her.

And that was when Robert, who had been anxiously hovering nearby, dropped the bomb that would change the direction of the war. "What'd you just call her?"

Trey looked blank. "What?"

Robert was a tower of puzzlement and accusation, looming over them. Kendra understood, seconds before he spoke again, and the nausea returned with a vengeance. "You called her Kendra." He looked at his wife for support. "He did, didn't he?"

Marlene was thoughtful, visions of grandbabies gone from her head. "He did, if I remember correctly." She looked from Kendra to Trey. Back at Kendra again. "Why'd he call you that?"

My skull. Hammers. Pounding.

"Natalie?" Marlene insisted. "Is that a…pet name or something?"

"No, it's…." Her eyes asked Trey *what now?*

Trey looked aghast, then resigned. He sighed. "Let's all have a seat. We can do this here or we can do it in the living room." He addressed his mother. "Where'd you be more comfortable?"

"Do what, son?"

Kendra hated the puzzlement on her face. Staring at the floor was the only way to avoid it.

Since nobody seemed inclined to pick a spot, he made the decision for them. "Here's good enough." He pulled out a chair right next to Kendra's. "Have a seat, Mom." For a minute, Marlene was fixing to play it stubborn. Then she got the drift that she wasn't going to like what she was about to hear, so she dropped abruptly into it.

"Pops?"

Soberly, Robert folded his arms across his chest. "I'll stand, if that's okay."

Trey nodded resignedly. "That's fine." The quiet hung in the room like a heavy cloud.

Finally, he released Kendra and rose, saying, almost to himself, "I think I'll have that drink after all."

"At this hour?" Marlene piped up almost automatically.

"Mom please, not now, okay?" He crossed to the cupboard and withdrew a new bottle of bourbon, holding it up to his father, who shook his head. He turned slightly, bottle still held aloft. "Kendra?"

Though she'd have committed a felony for a drink right now, she was too ashamed to answer to the name. Didn't even want to know how Marlene and Robert were reacting to hearing it a second time, spoken directly to her. She shook her head mutely.

Trey poured himself a glass, set the bottle down on the counter, and, holding it in both hands, sat next to his mother. He didn't take a sip.

"I'm waiting," Marlene said tightly.

He plunged in. "Mom, you remember the last time you were in hospital?"

"Course I remember. I had more tubes sticking out of me than a soda machine at a fast-food restaurant."

"Things didn't look good for you. We thought you were…" He struggled.

"About to get shipped across the river," she supplied with thin humor.

"Right. You remember what you told me?"

"I told you lots of things," Marlene hedged. Kendra could feel the older woman's piercing, curious and not exactly friendly gaze on her face. She hated it.

"You told me the one thing you regretted about…going… was not seeing me happy before you went. Remember? Not seeing me with someone new."

"I remember."

"What'd I tell you?"

"You told me you'd met someone. A girl called Natalie." Marlene's dark eyes, so different in color from Trey's, but just as discerning, didn't let up. "And this…isn't Natalie."

"No."

Marlene let her face drop into her hands. "You're cheating on your girlfriend? Shame on you, Trey. You should know better. And shame on you, too, young lady. Messing with another woman's—"

Could it get any worse, Kendra wondered.

Trey hastily derailed her train of thought. "No, Mom. I'm not cheating. There is no Natalie."

"Don't take me for a fool. You talked about her nonstop. About her e-mails. And your phone calls. How you were falling for her. Now you expect me to believe there's no Natalie?" She looked about to get up in disgust. "It's a good thing she's not here to hear you talk about her like that, poor child. Gives you her love, and this is what you do with it."

Robert pushed gently down on her shoulder. "Marlene, let the boy talk."

Earnest beads of sweat were popping up on Trey's forehead. "Mom, there really is no Natalie. I made her up."

Marlene peered intently at Kendra. "This person here, this woman, whoever she is, looks mighty real to me."

Trey briefly examined Kendra, as if weighing her realness. "She's real all right, but she isn't Natalie. Her name's Kendra, as you've probably figured out. She's a…"

I'm a what? Kendra wondered.

"She's a friend of mine."

"And what's with all the—" Marlene splayed open her hands. "All this Natalie stuff. Since I got here…all these lies?"

"You walked in on us. I wasn't expecting you. You turned up and caught me off guard. If I'd known you were coming, I'd have found a way to break it to you gently that Natalie was a lie. But you were standing there and I had to think fast."

"So you told me this girl was Natalie?"

"You *assumed* she was Natalie."

"Of course I assumed she was Natalie. You were kissing her, and your hands were everywhere." She turned to her husband. "You should have seen them, Robert, half-naked in the foyer."

Kendra gave a pained squeak.

"Mom," Trey said patiently. "Please, just listen."

"I don't understand. Obviously she's your girlfriend, so what's it matter what her name is? Why didn't you just introduce us properly and avoid all the lying? I'd have been happy either way, to see you with someone."

"The thing is," he explained uncomfortably, "she's not my girlfriend." Their eyes caught briefly, and Kendra closed hers to hide the pain. Trey went on. "She wasn't…she and I weren't involved—at the time."

"You looked mighty involved to me." Marlene gestured graphically, as if her husband needed an illustration. "All over her, I tell you," she repeated for Robert's benefit.

Even under these trying circumstances, Trey was doing his best to keep an even keel. "That just happened, Mom. Things like that happen between men and women."

Marlene sighed. "Well, who is she, then, if you're not 'involved'?"

Again, the glance from Trey. "Kendra and I had an…arrangement. A business arrangement—"

Marlene slapped her hands over her heart. "Oh my God! She's a hooker! Where're my pills?"

Trey's mother or not, Kendra really had to defend herself this time. "Oh, no, you didn't say that!"

Trey to the rescue, before things got nasty: "Kendra is *not* a hooker, Mom. Will you just listen?"

Mortification burned like a furnace in her cheeks. She ground her teeth to keep her words in. Better let Trey talk for me, she decided. Better not to say what I want to.

"Kendra used to work for me. At Wanderlust. Then I…she doesn't anymore. But we came to another arrangement. I asked her to come help me get the house set up, while she was searching for another job. That's all there was to it."

Marlene still looked confused. "And you made her pretend to be Natalie? Why?"

"I didn't *make* her pretend. The idea hit me when you assumed she was. So I asked her."

"Why?"

"I was afraid that if you found out the truth it would…"

"Kill me?"

He looked sheepish. "Something like that, yes."

"I'm stronger'n you think, boy," she said sadly. "Stupider, too, seems like."

Kendra hastened to assure her. "Marlene, nobody thought you were stupid. Trey was concerned for you, that's all. What with your health, and your argument with Robert, he didn't think you could stand the shock."

"I still don't understand. If the two of you aren't involved, then what's with all the…What about the way he looks at you? And the way you look at him? All the kissing." Her eyes narrowed. "Where were you last night, Trey, exactly? If you weren't really with…" she struggled with the name, still not used to it "…with Kendra?"

Trey answered delicately. "Kendra and I weren't involved *at the time*. When you got here, I mean. Not really. But since then things have…changed."

You could say that again, Kendra thought glumly. Things have changed so much I can't even believe this has all gone down in the space of a week. She stole a surreptitious glance at Trey's profile, remembering what had brought about this conversation in the first place. Discovering that she loved him. Had things changed anywhere near as drastically for Trey, too? Not likely.

"So, your make-believe romance suddenly got up and bit you on the butt? Are you involved now?"

What was he going to say? He took way too long to answer. "It's complicated." That was all. The man would play his cards close to his chest if it killed him. Disappointment was like bitter fruit in Kendra's mouth.

"Sure is." Marlene stood, groaning a little with the effort. When Robert rushed to help her, she didn't brush him away. She pressed her hand over her chest in a worrying manner. "Listen, son. Young lady. You need to excuse me. It's been a rougher morning than I was expecting—even with my husband turning up. Him, I'll deal with the way these things are supposed to be dealt with. In private."

Robert looked pained but patient.

Marlene went on, her deadly finger pointing again. "But you, you two! Y'all are more messed up than you think. You might have lied to me about your name, and you might have lied to me about a few other things, but I'm not an idiot. There's more going on between the two of you than you can even admit to yourselves. If you can't see that, well, God help you. But I've had enough. I need to go upstairs and lie down."

Kendra hated leaving it like this. God knew how Marlene felt about her now, this woman who kissed her in welcome every day, and who less than an hour ago was prattling cheerily on about seesaws and imaginary grandbabies. She rose and held out her hand to her. "Marlene, please, I'm so sorry. I can't imagine what you must think of me. You deserve to hate me for lying to you. But I want you to know I'm sorry."

Marlene didn't answer. Instead, she held Kendra in her long, considering gaze. Kendra felt like a bug staked down by a pin, fighting the urge to squirm. "Please, forgive me," she begged. It seemed she was always begging this family for forgiveness.

The lines in Marlene's face, which normally were parentheses around a huge smile, were deep ruts. Her lips and eyelids were tinged with shades of blue and gray. "I really need to rest." She steadied herself against the table, turned and headed out of the kitchen.

Robert, too, looked suddenly older, his youthful, energetic aura dimmed. He made to follow his wife. "I'll go make sure she's settled in. See that she takes her meds." He nodded at his son and then at Kendra. He looked almost as bewildered, hurt and upset as Marlene, but his Southern manners didn't allow him to leave without saying, "Miss, whatever your name is, whatever the circumstances, it's been a pleasure."

Kendra hoped she could hold back the tears of shame and humiliation until she no longer had an audience. She could only nod in response, afraid to speak, barely holding out until he left the room. Then the tears really did come. Big, sloppy, embarrassing ones, the kind that make you feel like you're five years old and you just wet yourself during your first piano recital. She wanted to get up and run, out the back, out the front, anywhere she could hide her streaked face from Trey.

But she couldn't move. Not because her knees were weak or her will insufficient, but because Trey was holding her. Even on his knees at her side, next to her chair, his head was level with hers. He tried to wipe away her tears, but he was clumsy and only succeeded in smearing her mascara. His tender attempts to clean up the mess only made things worse, so he gave it up and just held her until she was done.

Even after the hurricane blew itself out, he still kept on holding her. "Thirsty?"

She shook her head.

He got up and brought her a drink of water anyway. He placed it to her lips and she discovered she was parched. He held the glass for her, not allowing her to take it from his fingers as she drained it, and then put it down. The kitchen felt enormous, and in the middle of it the two of them were there, together, alone. Now, she had more to worry about than the reactions of Trey's parents. Now that they weren't here, clouding the issue and forcing explanations and apologies, the only thing Trey had to focus on was her. That made things dangerous. What if he guessed what she was feeling?

His own drink was still untouched. He placed his hand over hers. "You okay?"

"No."

He expelled air through his lips. "I'm so sorry. This is all my fault. I dragged you into this mess without thinking of what the consequences would be for you. That makes me a selfish bastard."

Don't talk about the man I love like that, she wanted to tell him.

"I'm sorry, Kendra. If anyone needs forgiving, it's me."

She eased herself out of his arms, even though it was like prizing herself away from a bonfire on a cold, wet night. "I guess I'd better—"

He panicked, getting up from his squatting position on the floor a little too fast. "What?"

"I'd better be leaving. I'm not exactly homecoming queen, as far as your parents are concerned. I'm lucky they were civil." She tried not to look in the direction of the stairs, in case they were hovering there like vengeful ghosts.

"They'll come 'round," he insisted. "Nothing fazes my father for long. He's a rock. And Mom'll be okay, once she's thought it through. I know her."

"Not as well as you think, evidently."

"But you still don't need to go." He was almost pleading.

Stay and face more humiliation? Never. Besides, as far as she remembered, they had a contract with set terms. Those conditions had been fulfilled, and her little improv acting job was over. She fumbled for her bag, and then hesitated over the gorgeous bunch of flowers. He'd bought them for her, and had presented them to her so tenderly. But as beautiful as they were, they were merely stage props for a travesty that had run its course. They weren't hers to take.

Trey followed her outside. "Kendra…"

She was so, so tired. If this needed to end, it needed to end cleanly. And clean meant fast. If he delayed her, there'd be no telling how soft her resistance would become, and that way lay trouble. "Trey, we had a deal. I was to pretend to be your girl-friend for two weeks, or until your mother knew the truth. She knows, so this is over. There's no more reason for me to stay."

The hurt on his face was like a stab to her heart. "There isn't?"

She shook her head. "Natalie's blown away like a puff of air. She's gone."

"Kendra's still here."

Oh, Lord, this really *is* complicated. There was so much she was feeling right now. Not just love, but fear. Fear that he'd find out she loved him commingled with the fear that he never would. Fear that his knowing would make her weak. "I have to go." The front gate seemed a thousand yards away.

He slid around her, blocking her path. Taking charge. His hands were on his hips in a gesture that told her he meant business. "I want to see you again. Tonight."

"Your dad flew in to see you. You should be spending time with him. With both of them. Take your parents out to dinner."

"Come with us."

Was he for real? "You saw what went on in there. You really think I'd be able to face them again? You think they haven't seen enough of me for one day?" She tried to laugh. "Besides, I'd hate to spoil their dinner, scarlet woman that I am."

"But this isn't over, you and me. It wasn't all pretend." His eyes were searching, dangerously perceptive. "Was it?" He looked afraid to hear her answer, but ready to deal with it, whatever it was.

"No," she answered truthfully. "But—"

Then her toes were off the ground as he lifted her up and spun her around once. "I knew it! I sensed it!"

"Trey!" She pounded him on the shoulder. "Put me down!"

Instantly, she was on terra firma again, but he was grinning. "I knew it wasn't all make-believe. I knew you felt something."

"But I don't think—"

He shushed her. "Wait. We need to talk, but doing it now won't do either of us any good. This isn't the right time. Or place. We've both had a rough morning. We need to regroup, sweetheart—"

Sweetheart? What was he trying to do, kill her? She tried again. Maybe he'd hear her this time. "I don't—"

He rushed on with the confidence of a chairman of the board handing down a decision that he expected to go unopposed. "My parents' cruise leaves in three days. If you need time to think, you've got it. But when they're gone, we're talking."

"Trey—" she began. Third time lucky? Nope. He kissed her lightly and sent her on her way.

Chapter 13

Forgiveness

The next three days passed at the speed of maple sap oozing down tree bark. Three days were more than enough time for Kendra to list all the reasons that, whatever Trey had in mind for them, she'd do better to talk him out of it. Because there was no way any romance between them was going anywhere. They were too different. They were both hauling around too much baggage.

He was a man of secrets, although many of his were now open to her. But she was a woman of secrets, and some of those she hadn't—and couldn't—share with him. They'd gone too far for her to go back to square one and start "splainin" herself. So it would be better for all concerned, including Marlene and Robert, if they were adult about this and just called it quits.

But in her moments of weakness, mostly at night when she was tossing, sleepless, in the bed she and Trey had shared twice, her determination slipped. She needed him, emotionally and sexually. When those moments were upon her, she struggled to keep herself from calling him up, confessing her love and begging him to come over.

And then in cold daylight, when she was sane again, she congratulated herself on her strength in not calling him, even though she knew damn well that that "strength" was just cowardice in disguise. But her respite was going to be brief. Trey was a man of his word, and that the moment his folks were en route to their cruise ship, he'd be making contact.

In that, she was right.

So there she was, seated across from him at his kitchen table, the remnants of a sumptuous meal lying before them. He'd ordered in from the Aegean Isles, the restaurant they'd been too chicken to enter on their first night out together.

She'd never been in his house at night. She appreciated the way the subtle, indirect lighting he'd installed changed the colors. The walls that glowed so sunnily in the bright light of day were now mellow, warm and welcoming.

Trey had dressed carefully, and he smelled of an aftershave she'd not noticed him wearing before. He had the smooth, put together look that signaled a great deal of effort, and she knew he'd done it for her. Dinner had been pleasant but guarded, as if they both knew there would be intense discussion in lieu of dessert, and they were pacing themselves.

He got up and cleared away the dishes, then poured her another glass of sweet Greek wine. Then he sat again, and cocked his head to one side, lips slightly curved. "Nervous?"

"Maybe a little," she admitted.

"Don't be."

"Are you?" she countered.

He laughed softly at himself. "I guess."

That surprised her. He was always so confident. So self-possessed. It made her feel a little better. "How'd things go with your folks?" she eventually asked, even though that was steering the conversation in a dangerously personal direction.

He weighed the question for several seconds, then said, "Pretty good. At least Mom was willing to suspend her skepticism and let Pops have the week to plead his case." He went on. "Things'll work themselves out. Deep down, Mom doesn't want to leave my dad. She's just been feeling blue lately, and needed a little attention."

"Sometimes you have to shout to get that," she commented.

"I guess sometimes you do."

She was afraid to ask, but she did anyway. "Did she say anything about me?"

He shook his head, but offered this comforting opinion: "She'll forgive you, Kendra. I promise." Then, as an almost inconsequential observation, he said, "You forgot to take your flowers."

Her mind was suddenly filled with the riotous image of pink tulips. "I wasn't sure they were really for me."

"What d'you mean? I gave them to you."

She explained herself. "Were they a show of affection for your father's sake, or did you really want me to have them? Were they for Natalie or for Kendra?"

"They were for the woman I made love with the night before."

There was that word again. Love. She looked away. She waited for him to speak again.

When he did, it wasn't about the flowers. "You know, that first night with you, I was scared out of my mind."

"I know."

"I told myself there were so many reasons not to sleep with you, but none of them held water. Or maybe they did, but there were forces in play that were stronger than those reasons."

She could feel her heart swell. "What forces?"

"Loneliness, I guess. That, and an awful hunger. I hadn't touched anyone or been touched in such a long time, I was like a famished dog let off his chain." Embarrassment and shame crossed his face. "I know I was greedy with you and only took what I wanted, and I'm sorry. I hope I didn't hurt you."

"You didn't," she confirmed softly. "Why are you—"

"Wait. Let me finish." As he held up his hand, his wedding band gleamed in the soft light. "Then I sneaked away. It was probably the most unmanly thing I've ever done. But I was disgusted with myself. And embarrassed and angry for breaking my fast."

"Why? You couldn't really expect to be celibate your entire life."

Idly, he toyed with his table napkin. "I don't know if I truly expected that, but I clung to the idea anyway. It became an obsession. It kept me focused and helped keep the pain away. I'd gotten dependent on my celibacy. I turned to it whenever I was in distress."

She knew what he meant. "Sort of like me and my eating."

"Exactly." He abandoned the napkin and focused on her again. "Next morning, when you came to the house, I felt so bad about myself I could barely look at you. I took the easy way out and ran."

"But you came back," she pointed out. "That same night."

"Yes." He smiled self-deprecatingly. "Still starving. Still needy."

"Any port in a storm, huh?" It hurt to think that all he wanted from her was the release that she could offer him.

"No, no! That night, I came back for something more."

She barely had the strength to ask, "What?"

"You."

She sat there, trying not to hope that he meant what it sounded like.

But he did. He elaborated, taking his time, as if to make sure she understood. "I'm still having a hard time getting used to it, because I honestly never asked for this. But I'm feeling things for you I haven't felt for any woman in a long time. And I have to be honest with you, Kendra, it's scaring the crap out of me. I feel like I'm being drawn and quartered by four wild horses. Logic taking me one way, my body taking me another. My heart, my soul…" He shook his head. "It's so confusing."

She should have been overjoyed at his revelation, and a part of her was, but the overarching feeling was one of compassion for the agony he was going through. She touched him on the hand. "I know this is hard. But believe me, Trey, you aren't betraying Ashia's memory. If she was everything you said she was, she's woman enough to let you go. And you need to let her go, too."

He shook his head. "Ashia's only half of it. I'm working on that. At least, I'm trying."

"It takes time."

"She was my world."

"I know." Oddly, she wasn't jealous.

"But she isn't what's bugging me right now. She's not what's standing between us. Because, I have to be honest, I want to be with you."

Did she have the nerve to admit she was feeling the same way? She did. "I want to be with you, too."

He smiled in relief and pleasure. "There's just one thing we need to get out of the way." He got up abruptly and came around to her, dropping to his haunches beside her.

He was so close, and all she wanted to do was lean forward and wrap her arms around his shoulders, but fear stopped her. "What?" she choked. What more was there to say?

"I need something from you."

"You need…" she began slowly, not understanding.

"Your forgiveness. You did something stupid, but I understand why you did it. But I was harsh and unkind and I hurt you. I judged you badly. I know that now. I'm sorry. Can you forgive me?"

She slid from the chair so she was on her knees facing him, hands placed on top of both of his. "Of course." She nestled her face in the crook of his neck, unable to bear the intensity in his eyes.

He hugged her back. "Kendra, baby, please. I know I'm clumsy, and I'm not doing this right. I'm rusty, dealing with women. Having a lover. Feeling like this. I don't remember how to say what I want to say. About what's going on in my heart. I wasn't asking for it. It took me by surprise. But it's real. Understand?"

Was he saying he loved her? Her heart was racing like the crowd favorite at the Kentucky Derby. She barely had breath to answer, "Yes."

Chapter 14

Love and Chocolate

She was glad that this time they were at his house, and not hers. Something different was going on between them tonight, and it was fitting that this new start would take place somewhere other than in her small, crowded apartment that held memories of their first painful, fumbling steps toward each other.

She stood in the middle of the living room as he moved about, happy and excited and full of love for him. Would he whisk her straight upstairs to his now vacant bedroom? Or would he lay her down on this huge couch, in the room where they'd first kissed, and make love to her right here? Both possibilities left her tingling with a mixture of excitement and trepidation.

He turned on the fireplace that he'd converted to gas, even though it was a fairly warm evening and they didn't really need it. The firelight licked the room and in its glow, the small statues, most of them African, danced for the new couple. The Somali painting, his wife's painting, was alive, watching them alertly.

"Anything special you want to listen to?"

"Uh…" *Your voice whispering in my ear,* she considered telling him. "I don't know. Whatever you like."

He hummed softly, withdrew a disk and slid it into the player. Nina Simone. She lifted her brows, both surprised and impressed. Then, with a magician's flourish, he produced out of nowhere a plain black box wrapped in a silver ribbon. He walked toward her, holding it out with a mischievous smile on his face. "This one," he told her, "is for Kendra. Not for Natalie or for anyone else."

"Tell me that's not a kinky sex toy," she cracked, with equal parts apprehension and expectation.

"Oh, it's sexy, all right." When she didn't take the box, he opened it and brought out a small, round ball of chocolate. "These are hand-made, seventy-five percent cocoa. Liqueur-filled. Thing is, they're assorted, and you don't know which chocolate has what liqueur until you bite into it." He pressed one between her lips. "Close your eyes and taste this."

She did as she was told, closing her eyes and cupping his hand in hers as he slipped it into her mouth. Heaven, heaven, heaven. This was *real* chocolate, not the kind you pick up at the 7-Eleven. She could taste bitter earth, wood and the most subtle hint of tobacco. The fragile shell broke between her teeth and flooded her mouth with orangey warmth. "Mmm. Grand Marnier."

"Is it?"

"Think so."

He bent forward and tasted her mouth, slipping his tongue between her lips to sip at the delicate sweetness. Lightning shot through her whole body, and grounded itself in her groin.

"I think you're right," he said contemplatively. He picked up another chocolate and delicately inserted it past her willing lips. "Let's see what we have here."

Kendra had a flashing image of herself standing in a hot, tropical field of cocoa trees, with their broad leaves wet from rain, brushing her face, and grass sticking to her bare feet. "Are these legal? Where'd you get them?"

"My secret. Now, bite."

She bit.

He was waiting.

She couldn't even open her eyes. "Mmm!" Even the air she exhaled was infused with the perfume of cocoa.

His mouth was near hers, like he was trying to share the perfume by proximity alone. "Don't keep me waiting. What is it?"

"Amaretto."

"Let me see." She felt one arm slip around her waist and pull her against him. He led her in dance, grooving them both into Nina's rhythm. Then, again, the bold tongue, tasting hers. Tasting the liqueur-drenched chocolate. "Right again."

They danced awhile. As they did, he held the box behind her in the hand that was around her waist. The stuff he was feeding her had to be eighty proof, because she was woozy. She struggled hard against the urge to melt into him, let her knees go soft under her so he had to bear her entire weight. She wanted to slide into sleep, right there in his arms, and let him dance her through her dreams.

She opened her eyes. His mouth was tinged with cocoa, and she knew hers must be, too. "Your turn."

She twisted around to get at the little black box and removed one of the devilishly deceptive, plain brown balls. Instead of transferring it to his mouth with her fingers, she held it carefully between her front teeth. Then, like a mother crocodile passing an egg to a surrogate, she slipped it to him in a kiss. "Better if you close your eyes," she advised.

"It always is, isn't it?" he murmured.

She waited. Watched him lick his lips. "Save some for me," she reminded him.

He bent forward and kissed her. At the same time, they said, "Crème de menthe!" and laughed with delight.

"This is a sin," she commented.

"I'll do penance later." They danced and kissed and kissed and danced. A few chocolates later he set the box down. "I think we're both past the legal limit."

"I guess we can manage to stay off the roads."

"I'm not taking you any farther than…" of one accord, they turned to the couch "….right about here." He set her down, pressing her back into the cushions and stretching out above her. Even after they'd kissed away the chocolate, they found their kisses were still unbearably sweet. He slipped the straps of her dress down until her breasts were bare to him, and then sucked gently on one nipple until her breath was coming fast and sharp between her teeth.

"Crème de cacao," he murmured. "Let's try the other one."

"Oh, Lord, Trey, I'm dying…"

"Shush. I've only just started." He took the other nipple between his teeth and teased it until she was using words that shouldn't be said in polite company. After a few long, sweeping licks, he made his pronouncement. "Sweet, coconutty Malibu." He smiled up at her. "You pack a hell of a kick, lady."

"Malibu, huh?"

"Mmm-hmm."

The glitter in his eyes was contagious. Points of wicked light were reflected in hers. "Sort of makes you wonder, doesn't it?"

"Wonder what?"

"What you taste like."

His swiftly drawn breath was reward enough for her audacity. He raised himself off of her, stood up and held out a hand. "Upstairs. Now."

Upstairs, in his big bed, Kendra discovered a delightful conundrum: their bodies were so closely intertwined, so literally joined at the hip that it would be a stretch of the consciousness to identify where one of them began and the other one ended. And yet, the feel of him, his scent, his taste, the sound of his groans and the dampness of his sweat were all so new to her that she felt as if she'd landed on foreign soil, and she needed to explore and map every inch of him with her hands and eyes and lips.

He was tireless, endlessly hungry for her body. Even when she was exhausted, he pushed her past her limits, or, rather, showed her how to expand them. Finally, somewhere in the vacuum in time between the point where night ended and morning began, he, too, gave up, and fell exhausted beside her, whispering her name. His mouth was against her ear, and through the matted curls of limp, wet hair, she heard him hoarsely say these words: "I love you."

She could have said so much at that moment, expressed her joy and gratitude, her awe that he was able to set his pain aside enough to let her into his locked heart. But she thought better of it, understood that he was too fragile for any of that. So she opened her eyes, catching his seductive, emotion-darkened gaze with hers, and said, "I love you." With his head pressed to her breast, he drifted off like a baby in his mother's arms.

When she woke up, she was alone, but the sound of the running shower stopped her from panicking. She lounged in the bed until he came out and began putting on a crisp, long-sleeved shirt and tie.

"Work, huh?"

He nodded. "I've been delinquent enough this week, what with taking my parents around. I've got a stack of paperwork on my desk so high, it'll be another week at least, before I get to the bottom of it. Petreena's probably half forgotten what I look like." He lifted his brows at her, waggling them like Groucho Marx. "Of course, I'd much rather be here with you."

She hurled a pillow at him that landed squarely on his belly. "Don't even think of it. I'm sore all over."

"You aren't the only one."

"And yet, you still want more?"

"Men are greedy." He put his pants on, then sat next to her on the bed and put on his socks and shoes.

She rolled over and kneeled behind him, rubbing his shoulders as he tied his shoelaces. The black leather was so well polished she could see his fingers reflected in them. "Well, you've had more than your fair share for one night, so get going."

In response, he twisted so he could kiss her. He hadn't repeated his assertion of love since that first time, but it shone unspoken in his eyes. He rummaged in the drawer of his nightstand and withdrew a small bunch of keys. "Here. Let yourself out with these. Keep them. Stick around as long as you want to. You could probably do with a little more sleep." At that, he twinkled. "Have breakfast before you go."

"You worked me up one hell of an appetite."

"I aim to please."

"Please you did."

His hand was poised over his pants pocket. "Do you need money to get around?"

The question was like a blow to the head. She was instantly serious. "No."

He was flustered, unsure. "I didn't mean that the way it sounded. I wasn't trying to imply…" He glanced behind her at the rumpled bed. "I was just thinking…things are rough with you right now."

"I know that wasn't what you meant." Her situation was dire, but there was no way she would accept money from him, especially not after the night they'd spent together. "I'm okay, Trey. Don't worry about me. I'll get by."

"I want you to do more than get by. I want you to thrive."

"I'll figure out a way to solve my problems. I can do it."

"I know you can, but what kind of man would I be if I don't help?" Then he added with a half-smile, "And you're in luck, kiddo."

What could possibly be lucky about her financial position?

"You've got a boyfriend with an MBA. Finance is my thing. Why don't we set aside some time to go over your books and try to figure out a way to get you out of this mess?"

Under any other circumstances, that offer would have been gold, but she hesitated. If she handed over things like bills, bank statements, personal documents, it was inevitable he'd find out more about her than she'd told him. Her last secret. What would he do then?

Maybe she should tell him now. Cast aside caution and take her medicine like a big girl. "Trey…" But she stopped. Why test the fragile strength of their relationship?

He continued, misreading the reason for her doubt. "We can do it, I promise. It'll take time and discipline. You'll have to sell some of your pretty things." He reached down and lifted her emerald bracelet from his bedside table, the one she'd been wearing the day he'd fired her. The one that had helped him form the horrible opinion he'd had of her in the first place. "But I'm sure you'll find that financial freedom is worth more than baubles like these. Trust me. I'll help."

"I'd like that," she choked. He was looking at her with such kindness and emotion that she made up her mind. The confession would come. But not this morning.

He nodded, glad she wasn't upset. "Good. Soon as you're ready, okay?" He kissed her on her forehead. "I'll see you when I get back?"

"I'll be here," she promised.

Chapter 15

And the Walls Came Tumbling Down

The next few days were wonderful. Trey was loath to leave her every morning, but she was waiting for him every evening when he came home from work; and every evening he had a new suggestion about something they could do together, from the silly to the erotic. One night they played strip Trivial Pursuit until one a.m. Another, he took her to see a local group's dramatization of James Baldwin's *Go Tell it on the Mountain*. That Saturday they went on a hike that, gentle as it was, had Kendra groaning from soreness before they were halfway through. That Sunday, they didn't bother to get out of bed. It was as though Trey was trying to cram all he'd given up over the past six years into a single week.

On Monday morning, she decided to surprise him by packing a picnic lunch and inviting him to De Menzes Park.

He'd done so much for her, paying for every activity and every meal, and although her finances were strained, she was determined to make this little outing one to remember.

She kissed him good-bye with a smirk on her face that had him guessing, and the moment his car was out of view, she leaped up and high-tailed it out of the house. She spent the next hour or so browsing through her favorite gourmet store, putting together a menu to knock his socks off. By eleven she had a spread that Emeril himself would have been proud of. Carefully trimmed rounds of French bread slathered with soft, herbed goat cheese and drizzled with olive oil. A salad of wild greens with a honey vinaigrette. Thin slices of duck breast with sorrel sauce, vegetable risotto and snow peas with a snap that could be heard across the room. Coffee cheesecake for dessert and a rich Chilean red wine to bring it all together.

She lined a basket with a red cloth and arranged everything inside. A fresh sprig of parsley draped over the edge—a whimsical touch to make him laugh. She hurried over to Wanderlust, anxious to be there before he left for lunch. If all this effort turned out to be wasted…!

Outside the Farrar-Chase building, the news vendor was in his usual spot at the newsstand. For some odd reason, she was surprised. She'd half expected that, during her three-week absence, there would have been drastic changes on Blackburn Boulevard: buildings razed and rebuilt, traffic rerouted, a helipad on the top of Farrar-Chase, that sort of thing. But it was as though she'd never been away. She wasn't sure if that was a good sign or not.

There seemed to be a thousand steps leading up to the main doors, and each one felt three feet high. True to his promise, Trey said he had cleared her name at the office, slipping a word into the gossip mill that the auditors had been mistaken, and that she had been wrongfully implicated. He'd manfully endured the whispers among his shocked staff that he'd made an awful mistake in letting her go.

Still, she was nervous about entering. It was impossible to shake the memory of being sent packing with a box in her arms, and of the stunned stares of coworkers who couldn't wait for the door to close behind her to begin their frenzy of gossip. Trey might have planted the seeds that would help resuscitate her good character, but that didn't mean she was scandal-free.

By the time she stepped out onto the sixteenth floor, she was beginning to feel a little foolish. If she walked in there with a cutesy straw basket, it would be obvious to all that she was involved with Trey. It would be hard enough for her to stand the talk, but what about him? Would his authority be undermined by the ensuing gossip?

But the die had already been cast. She pushed open the glass door to Wanderlust and stepped determinedly in. The receptionist at the front desk nearly choked on her frapuccino. "Oh, uh, Kendra!"

"Morning," she responded with enforced cheeriness. "How you doing, Marcia?"

"I'm, uh, fine." Not that she looked it, with milky coffee dribbling down her chin. "Can I, I mean, may I help you?"

"I'm here to see Trey Hammond."

"Oh." Marcia looked at the basket, seeming half-afraid that it might hold a weapon. Were they all going to wind up on the six o'clock news? "Is he expecting you?"

Kendra smiled sweetly. "Not exactly, but I'm sure he'll see me. Is it okay if I proceed?" And proceed she did, without waiting for so much as a yea or a nay.

Life being what it is, she'd barely made it inside when, who would she run smack into but Iris. "Kendra!" Iris, as usual, was all pink-faced and beaming and happy. She engulfed Kendra in a fluffy, gauzy embrace, allowing her to recognize that what looked like a ruby brooch on her collar was in fact a squished cherry Gummi Bear.

Strangely enough, she was happy to see Iris, too. "Nice to see you. How're your kids?"

Iris didn't need a written invitation. "Poor Zachary's teething."

"Is he?"

"Tooth number eleven, no less. That's way above his curve, you know. Fussy with it. You know how trying the whole teething thing can be." She rolled her eyes in fake exasperation and genuine maternal pride.

Kendra murmured appreciatively, even though she really didn't know how trying the whole teething thing could be.

"Doesn't stop him from being up to his mischief, though." Iris looked eager to tell the tale, and that spelled trouble. "Caught him with his daddy's nail clippers the other day. I keep telling Tony not to leave any sharp objects lying about, but he's worse than a kid himself. It all goes in one ear…. Anyhoo, my son takes the clippers, and trims all ten little piggies without cutting himself even once." She waited for Kendra's affirmation, but then, before it could come, added thoughtfully, "Although I did have to slap him on the back to make him spit out that mouthful of nail clippings."

It was time to get going. "Hey, Iris, I'm really happy to see you. We ought to, you know, do something soon. But I was going up to see, uh, Mr. Hammond."

"So you're coming back to work, right? Now that you're in the clear again." She shook her head sorrowfully. "Can't imagine how the boss could have made a mistake like that. Blaming you for that awful mess!" She hid her mouth behind her hand. "Everyone here was saying all sorts of stuff about you. But I always said you'd never do a thing like that. I *told* them!"

Nice to know Iris had such faith in her—that is, if Iris had actually overcome the temptation to join in on such a juicy chunk of gossip. "Thank you. But I think I'd better—"

Iris wouldn't take the hint. "You suing him?

"Of course not." That was a horrible idea.

"You could, you know. That's unfair dismissal, if I ever saw it. You could make lots of money. Tony's kid sister passed the bar last year. She'll work cheap. Want me to hook you up?"

"I'll let you know," she assured her, without speaking aloud the rest of the promise, which had something to do with airborne oinkers. "But it's getting late." She added, with a generous helping of mischief, "I'm taking Trey Hammond to lunch." She noted with satisfaction that Iris's gape was wide enough to park a station wagon in, and made good her escape.

On to Trey's office. She hitched up the picnic basket and crossed the busy floor in its direction. The man who invented open-plan workplaces had a lot to account for. She was as naked and exposed as a newborn hamster. As she sailed up the stairs—the scarlet woman returning—whispers followed her like the gentle hum of bees.

Petreena was bustling around outside her own little office, which was situated off the entrance to Trey's. Her beautiful, precariously high patent leather heels—which Kendra spotted as Choos from ten paces—sank into the carpet as she walked, and a half dozen gold bangles rattled. When she caught sight of Kendra, she froze, a manila folder in one hand and a bright red stapler in the other.

"Petreena," Kendra acknowledged.

The other woman was confused, cautious. "Kendra. How are you?"

Kendra wasn't all that sure. She was still stinging about the way Petreena had cut her loose. But she'd been seeking forgiveness from so many people lately, that she felt it was time to do some forgiving of her own. She smiled and hugged Petreena. "It's good to see you."

Petreena didn't return the hug at first, but then lifted her hands in a gesture that resembled an embrace, before stepping awkwardly back. "Kendra, I want you to know that the last time you called, I…I wasn't exactly nice to you." Petreena laughed, mocking herself a little. "I mean, *you* know that. What I'm trying to say is that *I* know I wasn't being nice, and I'm sorry."

"You were just doing your job."

"Maybe, but I… At the time, I thought you'd… Mr. Hammond says he was wrong about you. That you didn't really take the, uh, you know."

Again, being vindicated wasn't all it was cracked up to be. She rushed to close the subject. "It doesn't matter now. It's over."

Petreena looked anxious for that part of the conversation to be over, too. She asked hopefully, "Coming back to work?"

Kendra shook her head. "No, that wouldn't be a good idea. There's too much…unresolved stuff. You know?"

Petreena nodded understandingly. "Have you found something else?"

"No, but I'm looking." Which reminded her, as if she needed reminding, that the last thing she'd been doing, in fact, was looking. She'd been too taken up with Trey to sit down and peruse jobs online thoroughly. But at least Trey had fulfilled his final promise to her, to produce a glowing letter of recommendation. With that, she didn't think she'd have much trouble finding something—if she ever got up off her tail and set the ball rolling.

But Petreena believed her; she had no reason not to. "Good."

A blanket of silence settled down between them like dust from the Sahara. Kendra became aware of the weight of the basket on her arm. "I came to see Trey. I mean, is Mr. Hammond in?"

Petreena glanced in the direction of the glass office. "He's there, but…do you have an appointment?"

"No, I wanted to…uh…surprise him." Now she began to feel just plain silly.

Petreena's large brown eyes went to the basket, as though she was seeing it for the first time. They shifted to Kendra's face, and returned to the basket. "Oh. I see."

Kendra could feel herself blushing crazily. "Yes, well… Can I see him?"

Petreena hesitated, shifting a little to look at Trey's closed office door. Then she said, with a small, eloquent shrug, "I guess you can. But I have to warn you, he's not in a good mood today."

That was news to Kendra. He'd been in an excellent mood when he'd clambered out of bed this morning. She'd made sure of that. "He isn't?"

"Nope. Came in a little late, started sorting out backed-up paperwork, and then some kind of bomb went off. He's been snapping at everyone. Including me." Petreena looked at the door again, as if she expected to see smoke curling out from under it.

That was okay. She had what it took to cheer him up. Kendra smiled confidently. "Leave it to me. I came to take him out to lunch. Maybe he'll be in a better mood when he gets back."

From the shape into which Petreena twisted her lips, it was obvious she wasn't convinced. But she said, "I hope so, if only for my sake. Last time I tried to talk to him he seared a strip off me."

"Can I…?" She gestured toward the big glass door. From where they were standing, she could just about see the edge of Trey's desk.

Petreena moved her arm in a gracious arc. The bracelets jangled. "Be my guest."

As she walked through the door, she heard Petreena murmur, "Good luck."

Crossing the threshold into Trey's office, the same nauseating feeling she'd had the last time assailed her. She was overwhelmed by the memory of that awful morning—the exposure, the awareness of everyone's uplifted eyes on her from the floor below. She was pretty sure a few pairs were on her now.

But that was silly. Things were different. Last time, she was on her way to a beheading. This time, she was inviting her lover out to a long, romantic lakeside lunch. If that didn't lift him out of his black mood, nothing would.

He was standing behind his desk, not working. Twiddling a

pencil between his fingers and staring hard at it as though it was a wonder of engineering that he just couldn't wrap his mind around. His brows were almost touching, and he was so deep in concentration he didn't even notice she was there.

After several bewildering moments of feeling invisible, she ventured to make a small sound, more of an exhalation than a word of greeting, just to draw his attention to her presence. It worked; he looked up. His face was expressionless, unmoving. Reflecting nothing.

In spite of this, she still hadn't cottoned to the fact that she was in the presence of grave danger, like a kid who had clambered down into a panther's cage at the zoo, and was standing there, cooing, "Here, kitty, kitty." She was all smiles. "Hi, darling."

Her smile was not returned. "What're you doing here?"

She was momentarily halted by the chill in his eyes; but like someone hit in the shoulder by a low-caliber bullet, rather than through heart by a hollow point, she was able to keep going. "I came to surprise you. I thought we could—"

"You're full of surprises, that you are."

Slow on the uptake she might be, but stupid she was not. Like a narrow orange light on the black horizon, the dawn of realization broke. It was possible—unlikely, perhaps, but possible—that she wasn't simply an innocent bystander stumbling onto the firing range. It was possible that this unfathomable anger, which stood between them like a wall of hot ice, might be directed at her.

Her smile faded. "Trey?"

He didn't look at her, but gestured toward the object clutched in her hand. "What the hell's that?"

She looked down at her hand, and, what'dya know, there was a basket attached to it. A few seconds of confusion in the face of such palpable hostility had been enough to erase it from her mind. "It's, uh, a basket." *And the winner of the Obvious Statement of the Year Award goes to…* "I mean, it's a picnic basket. I thought you might like to run out to De Menzes Park and have a little…" She trailed off miserably. His face told her that further explanations were both unnecessary and unwelcome.

"You did, did you?"

"Trey, what's going on?" She felt like a little girl who'd somehow managed to make Daddy mad, but couldn't understand why he was mad or what she could do to make things better.

"You don't know what's going on?" he challenged scornfully.

Her response was a wordless shake of the head.

The lips that had nibbled at hers a few hours before curled in disbelief and contempt. "Want me to tell you, then?"

She was sure she wouldn't like it, but whatever it was, it would be better than the awful pain of not knowing.

He glanced behind her, through the glass walls, onto the floor below, and cursed viciously. "I'm going to get this damned glass torn down and replaced with Sheetrock. A man's entitled to privacy in his own office." He stabbed at the intercom with the pencil. "Petreena."

Petreena answered as if she were hovering near the intercom, waiting for a summons. "Mr. Hammond?"

"I'm borrowing your office."

"Certainly, sir."

"You go on ahead and have lunch."

"Um, yes, Mr. Hammond." She was out of there in a flash of tangerine.

He crooked an imperious finger in Kendra's direction. "This way. You may thrive on scandal, but I don't care for an audience."

Her mouth fell open. "I thrive on *what?*"

Trey hadn't bothered to wait for her to get moving. He was already standing in the doorway of Petreena's office, arms folded. "You coming?"

She followed, her heart as heavy as the basket—and that weighed a ton. She wished she could open up a window and

hurl it outside. Too bad for whoever was passing by, sixteen
stories below.

His expression was murderous, a tornado bearing down on
her, deadly and unavoidable. Buy why? *Why?*

Once she was inside, he slammed the door. The force of it
rippled around the room. Petreena's office was a symphony of
pink. There was a shelf lined with dolls, from Limoges china
ballerinas in graceful poses to Bratz dolls with their navel rings
exposed. Even the pens and pencils in Petreena's little pencil
cup sprouted feathers and silk flowers at their tips. Strange
place for a war, Kendra thought. Especially one as bizarre and
unexpected as this one. But if there was going to be a war, she
was entitled to know what she was fighting for. "Trey, please,
please explain to me—"

His nostrils flared like a mad bull's. "*I* owe *you* an explanation? That's funny. I was thinking it should be the other
way around."

"But I don't even know why you're mad. When you left
this morning—" When he'd left this morning, he'd kissed
each of her toes, and promised them, in all seriousness, that,
if they were good little girls, he'd be back after work to kiss
them again.

"When I left this morning, I was ignorant of the facts, and dumb
enough to let myself be a pawn in whatever game you're playing."

"What facts?" But by now she was beginning to have a clue.
It was way past dawn now; the glaring light of understanding
filled the sky. Oh, damn, damn. He knows the truth.

A small, insignificant thing on the scale of the world, but it
must seem like such a huge thing to him. However he'd found
out, it had taken him by surprise. And what an ugly surprise it
must have been. All her fault. She should have said something.
While she had the chance, she should have.

He was taking up all the space in Petreena's office, out of place
in the midst of all that pink. The rage swirling around him made

his corner darker. His anger made the pink fade to gray. "Fine, you want to play dumb? Let's do it your way. You remember that heap of paperwork I've had on my desk this past week?"

She nodded, scared to say anything, in case even the sound of her voice made him madder.

"Know what was at the bottom of that heap?"

She couldn't say for sure, but she had a pretty good inkling. She waited for him to confirm her suspicions.

"A report. From my auditors. A follow-up report on the little magpie that had been stealing from me. I commissioned a further investigation into your background on the day that I justifiably kicked you off my premises."

Deep in her head, there was a loud rumbling sound. The sound of walls crashing down. "Trey…"

"Know what they found?"

Did she ever. Wearily, she let the basket slip to the floor. The bottle clinked as it rolled out, but didn't break.

His cynical smile did the impossible: it made him ugly. "I thought you would."

"I can explain."

"Would you like to see it? Or would you just like me to read it for you?"

"That won't be necessary."

"Fine. Let me lay the essence of it on you. Would that be okay, *lover?*" The last word sounded like poison.

The tornado again. And this time she was swept up in it, powerless in the face of its strength. There was nothing she could do but wait and let him vent.

"Apparently, Kendra Forrest doesn't exist. Which is interesting, if you really look at it. Because I just spent the first half of the past two weeks making it with a woman named Natalie, and the second half with a woman called Kendra. And neither of them is a real person!" In his rage, he was no longer recognizable as the man who was making love to her this morning, the man she loved, who'd cussed like a sailor when the alarm clock had gone off and he'd had to leave her.

"I'm real," she pleaded. "You know I am."

He shook his head emphatically. "You're a fraud. You're a lie." He laughed harshly. "The ghost that's been lying in my bed these past six years is more real than you."

Somewhere, Ashia must be smiling. Kendra had had the temerity to pit her wiles against a heart's memory—and she lost.

She tried reason. "You know I'm real," she insisted. "You've touched me and tasted me. You were on me this morning. In me. Don't you remember?"

He faltered, but pressed on as though he didn't want to be dissuaded. "Don't sidestep the issue."

"That *is* the issue. The only issue. I love you. You love me." Let it still be true!

"And who might *you* be? Other than the ballsiest, most conniving little con-woman I've ever come across. How much were you planning to squeeze out of me before you went on your way?"

Oh, he was tripping now! What she'd done was wrong, but there was no way he was going to brand her a thief—again. Not for something she didn't deserve. "I never took money from you. You offered me once, remember? And I refused."

"Yes, you refused. Maybe that was your strategy. Why accept forty, fifty bucks, when you could lay low and reel in a whole lot more?"

"How? Why?"

"Oh, I don't know, honey," he drawled nastily. "You aren't the first woman to go fishin' for a lonely widower. I'm sure if you'd managed to land me you'd have made a tidy little bundle. Hang around for a few years, file for divorce, and walk away grinning. You get half of a man's earnings in this state, don't you?"

She denied it heatedly. "I was not trying to land you, as you put it. I was not trying to…" She stopped when what he was saying fully hit home. "Who said anything about marriage?"

He laughed again, and this time the ugly sound was directed at himself. "See how much you had me fooled? See how deep into your trap I'd fallen?"

"Oh," she breathed. She was blindsided by the revelation. Trey had been planning to ask her to marry him.

Chapter 16

Fat Kat's Revenge

"My God." For Kendra, the exhalation was partly a prayer of thanksgiving. He'd loved her enough to want her to share his life! And it was partly a lamentation; he'd surely changed his mind since then, and that loss was without measure.

Trey sneered. "Oh, don't try to act like you didn't know. You made a fool of me. And you enjoyed every minute of it. I'm just glad your games in the sack didn't sucker me into completely abandoning my duties. Were you hoping you'd keep me there long enough for the report, that little fact you neglected to mention, to disappear? Did you think it would fall into a drawer somewhere and never be seen again?"

She had to defend herself against his absurd allegations. "I didn't try to keep you out of the office. And if I played any games *in the sack,* as you so crudely put it, I played them with your full consent and approval. And I played them because I love you!"

"Oh, please. Don't go giving love a bad name. I caught your act. You can drop it now."

She pleaded for her love, even though she knew that the truth would be lost on him. "It wasn't an—"

He wasn't even listening. "How many men have you done this to?"

"What'd you say?"

"You heard me. How many fools have you suckered like this? And for how much money? The businessman in me wants to know. What's your average take per man?"

Her response was instinctive, if a little idiotic. She wanted to throw something at him, and throw something she did, although if she'd had time to think, she'd have selected a more aerodynamic missile. But she was mad as hell, and the first thing her hand closed over was the sprig of parsley, which she flung at his chest. But she was a girl, and she threw like one. It bounced off him and flopped onto the table, looking sublimely ridiculous. She was sorry it hadn't been the bottle of Grey Poupon.

"I have not 'done this', as you put it, with anyone else, and this wasn't a con job. If you'd get down off your big, high, offended horse for ten seconds, you'd see that. And furthermore, I had no way of knowing there was any report in the first place. How was I to know you'd sicced your spies on me?"

"Due diligence, my dear. A basic tenet of good business. Something you should have thought of when you set me up in your little scam."

"For the last time, Trey, I didn't set you…" She covered her face with her hands. Protesting was pointless.

He wasn't ready to end the conversation. "I still can't figure out a few things. How'd you get this job with a fake Social Security number and fake ID?"

The storm of rage and pain and misunderstanding that they'd

been sucked into was making her weak. To conserve energy, she kept her answer dull and emotionless. "Shel never bothered checking. He liked me, so he hired me."

"A misplaced trust."

"That's not fair!"

"So, you skated under the radar with fake papers. Fine. But I'm still confused. There's one more thing you've got to sort out for me, *sweetheart*." Again, a term of endearment honed into a weapon.

She sighed. "What?"

"Who the hell is Kate Ford?"

Her vision was dimming. Everything around her seemed blurred. Wet. "A sad, lonely, fat, funny-looking kid who didn't like herself much. Somebody who changed what she didn't like, and then left as much of that ugly baggage behind in Gary, where it belonged."

"So, let's get this straight, you slimmed down, buffed up, left home and just wiped yourself off the face of the planet?"

"All I did was change my name."

"Legally?"

"No. I was planning to, but there wasn't much time. This job came up, and I needed papers fast. So I had them faked. And then, once I'd settled down here, changing it legally would have raised all these questions."

"So who's Kendra Forrest?"

"Me. I'm Kendra Forrest." She patted her chest emphatically.

"I meant—"

"I know what you meant. I haven't stolen anyone's identity. There's no other Kendra Forrest. It's just a name I liked."

"So you started wearing it, like a jacket you shoplifted in a store."

"I didn't want to be Fat Kat anymore."

"Who?"

"The girl in the photo. On my fridge. Remember?"

"Mm-hmm."

"That's what they called me all through school. That's what I started calling myself. Fat Kat. Kate didn't have any meaning for me anymore. It only reminded me of the shame and the teasing. The awful loneliness. So I killed her and became someone else." He had to understand that, didn't he?

He shook his head. "I was wrong."

Oh, sweet relief. He understood. This storm would pass, and things would go back to the way they were. Maybe they, as a couple, would even be better for it. She touched him on the arm. "I'll make it up to you, I promise. We'll get over this."

He didn't even seem to know she was touching him. He was talking to himself more than to her. "I was wrong to believe I could start again."

Was he even thinking that? She had to change his mind—fast, before his uncertainties set like concrete. "You weren't wrong! People aren't meant to be alone. Life's too short to even try."

She could tell he was weighing what she said. At least she'd managed that much. But his next words told her that she'd been weighed, measured and found wanting. "Then maybe I was just wrong to think I could start again with you."

Slap, slap. Her face couldn't have stung more if his blows had been physical. From across the years, Fat Kat laughed mockingly. *Wanted to kill me, did you? Wanted to bury me and pretend I never existed? Think again. I'll be with you all the days of your life.*

He pulled up their conversational drawbridge, the last thing that connected him to her from across the wide moat of their misunderstanding. "You need to go."

"Go?" she repeated stupidly.

"You heard me."

"But where? Home? What have I got to go home to? Nothing. Nobody. You're all I've got." She could hear how pathetic and desperate she sounded, but didn't care. "Where d'you want me to go, Trey?"

The transformation from lover to stranger was complete. She wasn't even sure if he was seeing her anymore. He stepped out from behind Petreena's desk, passed her, and was already heading back to his office. "Get out of my business, Kendra, Kate, whoever you are," he flung at her without even glancing her way.

Frozen, she stared at his back.

Then, as he placed his hand on the door handle, he stopped, struck by a thought. He half turned. "Before you go…"

"Yes?" Hope dared to raise its head.

"I'm going to need my keys back." It was as if he had smashed Hope's head with a rock.

Kendra fumbled in her pockets, hands so cold and nerveless she could barely grasp the small bunch of keys to his house, which had been a symbol of trust and sharing. She dropped them, leaned forward to recover them, and stopped.

Grow some backbone, her last shred of self-esteem scoffed. *He wants his keys? He can damn well come back over and pick them up himself.* She straightened up and glared at him.

He looked down at them, then across at her, and got the message. The first person to go for those keys lost. He wasn't even willing to play the game. He spun around and stomped into his office, coming pretty close to shattering the door as he slammed it behind him.

Chapter 17

Redemption

Days passed slowly. Painfully. Kendra cried a whole lot and ate very little, which was mildly surprising. The not eating part at least, not the crying part. Just weeks before, when she'd suffered her first humiliating ouster at Trey's hands, she'd buried herself under a comforting avalanche of food. The fact that she hadn't even felt the urge to throw herself a chocolate-covered pity party was proof she was finally getting the better of the dreadful food addiction that had made her young life such torment.

But there were other problems to be faced, and the most pressing one was staring her right in the face: money. If she didn't do something soon, she'd be curled up on a street corner with her few valuables stacked behind her in plastic shopping bags.

"You're lucky you have a boyfriend with an MBA," Trey had told her, way back in the ancient history of last week, when he still considered himself such. At the time, his offer had brought her panic rather than comfort. If she'd taken him up on his offer then, she'd have had to explain why the name "Kate Ford" kept turning up on so many of her financial documents. So she'd thanked him, but conveniently kept forgetting to bring him her paperwork.

Kendra squeezed her eyes shut in regret. The problem had seemed insurmountable, but the solution—coming clean—had been so simple—yet she hadn't had the guts. He would have understood, she was sure of it; and he'd still have been by her side today. Trey was out of the picture now, permanently. She'd have to solve all these problems herself. The thought made her hyperventilate, but after she rode that wave for a minute or two, she went about the house, rummaging through drawers and handbags, collecting her bills and notices. Rent and credit cards, insurance and utilities. Overdrafts, late payments… She spread them all out on the table—there were so many of them— and then sorted them into heaps by priority. A horrifying number of them were stamped "Past Due."

She tallied up her debts. "Yikes," she said aloud when she was done, although, to be honest, the figures merited a response far more colorful than that.

Next up: her assets. Trey had suggested she sell her jewelry and other valuables. He'd been right. She didn't need all that stuff, anyway. She walked across to her dressing table and opened the half-dozen jewelry boxes that littered it. As she picked up the first bauble, a strand of pinkish pearls with a clasp shaped like a dragonfly, she hesitated, but only briefly. What needed to be done needed to be done quickly. She filled her hands with whatever she thought was worth something, in- cluding the emerald bracelet that Trey had responded to with such scorn.

She placed them all into a sturdy box and set them aside. Next, her clothes. She raided her closet with the determination of a storm trooper, and laid her old companions, who'd bolstered her self-image so much when she most needed it, out on the bed. She spread out dresses she'd put on when she was ready for war, and dresses she'd worn when she was craving attention. Jackets that made her feel like a million bucks. Gowns that had made the ugly purple monstrosity she'd worn to the prom seem like a figment of her imagination.

Her passionate love for them, each with the unique hallmark of its designer as clear to her knowing eye as a rubber stamp, would not allow her to sell them, even though she needed the money. These, she decided, were going to Goodwill, where some other woman, who was worse off than she, could find them and take joy in them. The idea of it made her smile and brought her some small measure of redemption. Go with God, Vera. Dolce and Gabbana, nice to have known you guys. Hermès, give my regards to the folks in Paris.

By the time she'd packed everything up into wheeled suitcases, she was emotionally and physically drained. Seeing her stuff go would be like releasing a pod of young orcas back into the wild after having reared them by hand, but she'd resigned her soul to the task.

She had to haul her bags downstairs, across three blocks, to the nearest busstop, and wait for a downtown bus, looking like a tourist or a runaway. Even dragging two suitcases at a time, the exercise took several trips into the city, spread out over a day and a half. The jewelry, as she expected, brought in a fair amount of money; they alone were enough to cover her back rent. When she was done with her shoes and handbags, she was assured that her power and phone weren't going to be cut.

Now, to lead herself not into temptation. When she was sure there wasn't a single saleable item left in her small apartment, she stood barefoot on the floor, where a reasonable imitation of a Persian rug had once lain, and turned her credit cards into confetti. Satisfying, but not good enough. She had accounts with many department stores and fashion outlets, and knowing that they were still out there, open, waiting for her to go charge something again, was going to keep her up nights. Late on the afternoon of the second day of her economic siege, she made her third trip into town, and visited each of her old haunts in turn to inform them, politely but firmly, that she wanted a divorce.

She hit Nordstrom's, Victoria's Secret, Macy's and Ann Taylor stores. By six-thirty she still had four more stores to go, but it was getting late. She was exhausted, and her arms ached from having dragged suitcases around, but her heart was as light as a helium balloon. She really ought to call it a day; she could hit the other stores tomorrow. Dinner, a shower and an early bed were a bus ride away.

But as she headed for the bus stop, a colorful sign caught her eye: Sweet Pickle, a favorite haunt of hers. It was a trendy fashion spot that attracted many of Santa Amata's black and Latina women. A little pricey, perhaps, but, oh, it had impeccable taste. Maybe she should pop in, do the needful, and be back outside in time for the bus…

…which was pulling up this very second. It hissed in greeting as the pneumatic doors swung open. Kendra moved forward and prepared to board. She was drop-dead tired. Sweet Pickle would have to wait until tomorrow.

But it was almost as though her addiction to shopping had been replaced by her overwhelming urge *not* to shop. She needed to cut herself loose from them—tonight. Free herself of the covetousness their glorious merchandise inspired in her. She tried, but her legs wouldn't let her get on that bus. The driver gave her a scowl, and the doors hissed shut again. She hurried across the street.

The interior of Sweet Pickle was as welcoming as Grandma's house, but a whole lot more swanky. As she passed the sale rack, the first thing she laid eyes on was a low-cut evening gown that flowed like pink Champagne. She reached out to stroke it, just to touch it, nothing else, and then withdrew her hand and stuck it into her jeans pocket.

She walked purposefully past the seductive lights and tasteful layouts, avoiding temptation by staring straight ahead and choosing a route that kept her as far as possible from the displays of her favorite designers. There was a desk near the back where she figured she could get the deed done quickly, and then hurry back outside to catch the next bus. Simple.

Not so simple. She was second in line, and something told her the woman in front would be a while. She was an exceptionally tall, dark-skinned sister, with a weave that fell past her waist. Her nails were hand-detailed—red butterflies on a white background, and her chunky bracelets clanked as she waved her hands in the air. "I don't know what you people have come to," she was saying. "I go out of town for a month, and first thing I do when I get back is come check out my homegirls at Sweet Pickle. Expecting you to hook me up with something special, know what I'm saying? I come here looking for you to blow me away, and what do I get? Nada. Nothing new. You guys used to be cutting edge. What happened?"

The woman behind the desk, much older, but stylishly dressed, looked pained. "Wanda, I understand what you're saying, but—"

"Last time, I dropped two grand in here, remember? You know me. I don't do cheap."

"I know, Wanda, and I'm really sorry. We're always grateful for your patronage, but—"

"But what? What is this?" She waved a blouse under the other woman's nose. "Where'd you guys get this crud from? You smuggle it in on a banana boat? Is this all the rage in Guatemala?"

Wanda was obviously an important customer, because the woman didn't even show a flicker of irritation. "Believe me, I understand. But our buyer, Shawna, quit on us a few weeks ago. Since then, we've been having trouble getting new merchandise in. We're trying really hard to find someone suitable, but it's not all that easy."

Kendra looked around with fresher, more enlightened eyes. The luscious displays were laid out to disguise the empty shelves behind them. The lighting that turned the store into a mysterious, sexy hideaway did double duty by hiding unstocked corners. Now she knew, it was easy to spot. Sweet Pickle was in trouble. Sad, really. She loved this store. It catered to her own personal sense of style so closely that it almost seemed as though they existed for her and her alone.

"We've put ads in the papers," the woman was explaining to Wanda, who hadn't put down the offending blouse, but who was listening with one hand on her hip. "But we haven't found anybody who's really into the Sweet Pickle philosophy."

"And that would be…?" Wanda challenged.

"They don't just have to know about fashion. They have to breathe fashion."

Ding, ding, ding! Sometimes the universe really was on your side. "Excuse me," Kendra piped up. "I don't mean to be rude, but…"

Both women stared at her as if they'd only just discovered she was there. Two pairs of brows arched. "Yes?" asked the woman behind the counter.

"I know a whole lot about fashion," she began, willing herself not to give in to the intimidation that radiated off the women. "I love clothes, I really do. And I do breathe fashion. I—"

Two pairs of eyes took in her old sweatshirt and her faded pair of jeans, and then rose to her makeup-free face, taking in her earlobes and throat unadorned by jewelry. They didn't need to say anything to be heard.

Kendra looked down at herself, mortified. "I know I don't look it, but, I, uh…" She what? Just gave away all her clothes? That'd sound great. "I was in town running a few errands. But usually, I…" This was ridiculous. She was starting from a position of weakness, not from one of strength. She rectified that. "I'm an old customer. If you check, you'll see a hefty charge account in my name. I know about clothes, and I know about jewelry. I've worked in sales before, and I know how to treat customers. I know how to sell ideas." She looked around at the empty shelves and added, meaningfully, "I know exactly what Sweet Pickle needs. Me."

The woman behind the desk considered her for a long minute. Wanda regarded her with frank curiosity, the amused smile on her face fading when she realized how serious Kendra was.

"Do you have a resume?" the woman asked.

"I'll have it for you in the morning," Kendra replied. Then she added, with the authority and spirit that the old, pre-Trey Kendra would never have had, "When I show up for work." She left both women gaping, and sauntered victoriously out of the store.

Chapter 18

Meet Me in Paris

Summer took Kendra by surprise. She was so busy with her new job, working so hard to ensure that at the end of her probation, Naomi, her employer, would keep her on, that she failed to notice the change in the weather. She didn't notice how the trees had broken into flower. She didn't notice that, with school out, the streets were thronging with children and teenagers searching for something fun to fill their empty hours. It all came to her one day. She opened her eyes, truly opened them, and, boom, it was summer.

Two months had slipped past since she'd seen Trey. At least, it had been that long since she'd been in his physical presence, because the man was never far from her in spirit. It was a haunting. Sometimes, she woke up on the other side of midnight and discovered her bed was empty, which surprised the hell out of her, because moments before, in the depths of sleep, she'd been in his arms.

She avoided Blackburn Boulevard, where the Farrar-Chase building stood, as though there'd been eyewitness reports that the streets were full of rabid rats. The possibility of bumping into him was too enormous. In spite of this careful avoidance, though, she was sure she spotted him once, in a crowd, walking away from her. In deference to the rising temperatures, he'd shed his heavy overcoat and was wearing just a long-sleeved shirt. He looked thinner. He never looked back, but for several minutes after he was out of sight she was unable to move—rocked, shaking, breathless.

And then, in early July, when she was in the tiny nook at the back of Sweet Pickle that passed for an employee lunch room, reading the paper, a small obituary caught her attention. It was accompanied by a full color photo of a woman. The bright, laughing brown eyes caught hers. Marlene. Kendra dropped the paper with a soft cry. Trey's mother had passed away peacefully in her sleep beside her husband. She'd been buried in her Georgia hometown on Saturday.

She was cut deep by grief. She'd loved Marlene, with all her spirit and her sharp tongue, her sense of fun and interfering ways. And then with her grief came shame. The last time she'd been in the presence of this beautiful soul, Marlene had been too angry to speak to her. And now she'd never know if she'd been forgiven.

Kendra allowed herself to grieve, trying not to connect the bitterness she felt toward the son with the pain she felt over the loss of his mother. She sent flowers to Trey, with a card that simply said, "My deepest sympathies, Kendra." She Googled Robert, found his address, and sent a second set of flowers with a card that said the same.

Several days later, a small white envelope arrived at her

apartment. She recognized the handwriting immediately and tore it open. Inside was a plain white card that bore Marlene's name and dates of birth and death. It had obviously been prepared for Trey to acknowledge expressions of sympathy from his friends and well-wishers. She flipped open the card. Two words, scrawled in black ink, took up most of the limited space therein: "Thank You."

Paris!

It boggled the mind. Only yesterday Kendra had been in boring old Santa Amata, sweltering in the August heat. Today, here she was in glorious Paris, she gloated to herself, and in Le Marais district no less, where the trendy people hung out. It was just as hot here, and just as sticky, but she'd rather sweat here than back home any day.

So far, her adventures as a buyer had been limited to forays into New York City and Miami; but with Naomi's steadily growing faith in her came greater responsibility. Now, Naomi had decided to let her spread her wings a little farther. It was a tremendous opportunity. Browsing through the boutiques and clothing markets, picking up stock for Sweet Pickle. Soaking up the experience of a lifetime. Couldn't beat that with a stick.

Her hotel was a quirky mix of the old and the new—like Le Marais itself. The building was several hundred years old, and her room nestled in a gable. In one corner, the roof slanted so low she had to dip her head to get to the bed. Antique willow furniture was re-covered in modern damask, and a porcelain bowl of fresh fruit sat on the table in the minuscule breakfast nook. Near the window, a small blue bird perched in its cage, looking out onto the medieval streets below and whistling happily. As entranced as she was by the whole setup, she had her reservations about the bird. Was she expected to clean up after it? And what if it sang all night?

She wasn't placing any bets that her schoolgirl French would be sufficient to convey her concerns, but she was sure going to try. She'd ask the young man who'd first brought her up to her room this afternoon—what was his name again? Jean-Henri. At least his English was better than her French, and he was almost overly helpful. He'd already turned up at her door three times, once to bring her fresh linens, once to bring in the bird, and once to ask if she was okay. She'd just have to call downstairs—

A knock made Kendra jump. Jean-Henri was attentive and intuitive, but that was downright scary. "*J'arrive!*" she yelled as she hurried to the door. "Coming!" With a tourist's typical disregard for safety precautions, backed by the belief that everyone left their doors unlocked in Europe anyway, she wrenched open the door without bothering to use the peephole, a smile of welcome on her face. Maybe he was bringing her a complimentary plate of warm buttered croissants. That'd be so cool….

Trey was standing there.

She screamed, leaped back and slammed the door so hard the little brass crucifix hanging on the inside clattered and fell. She slapped her hand over her mouth to keep from screaming again. Trey? Here in Paris? Here, in the same district of Paris, in the same hotel she was staying in? Not likely. The haunting had become too real. She'd finally lost her mind.

The knocking came again; two short raps, just as before. Trey *was* there. Shock. Elation. Anger. Fear. Should she open it? She was pretty sure she'd stopped breathing.

"Kendra, please." His voice was muffled through the dense wood. "Open up."

She placed her hand on the doorknob, but didn't turn it. Her stomach was roiling.

"Kendra?"

She was afraid to answer, in case the effort woke her up. Because if she did wake up, she might discover she was not in

Paris, but in her boring old apartment in her boring old bed, and that Trey was most definitely not outside her door. And furthermore, he still hated her.

That was the problem. Trey hated her. Despised her; had nothing but contempt for her. Believed she was nothing more than a thief and a con artist, some sort of serial prostitute who slept with men and beguiled them out of their money. And that memory was enough to force her dominant emotion to rise to the surface. Anger. Backed up by its lieutenants, Hurt and Suspicion, it was ready for war. She wrenched open the door. "What're you doing here? What d'you want?"

He hadn't moved a muscle. Both hands were loose at his sides. His shoulders sloped a little, surprising in a man who usually held himself so square. His head was bent slightly, his hair longer than she'd remembered it. Behind his thin glasses, those deep gray eyes were as dull as a stagnant river reflecting an overcast evening sky.

To say that she was shocked by his appearance would have been an understatement. But shock was not enough to soften her resentment, which was rapidly encasing her in a force field against pity. She repeated her question. "What d'you want, Trey?"

"To come in, for starters." Even his voice lacked the vibrant timbre she heard in her dreams.

She had half a mind to balk at his request, but something told her if she didn't accede he'd topple over in the hallway. Which would have brought on a host of other problems. How did you say 9-1-1 in French?

She let him in, keeping a wary eye on him, as if she half-expected him to do something sudden and scary. But he walked so slowly, with the gait of a defeated man, she was sure that "sudden" wouldn't describe anything he'd be doing. She closed the door, and this time locked it. Let that be the last unexpected visit she'd be getting for the evening. He stood uncomfortably in the center of the room. The low ceiling seemed even lower with him there. He turned and glanced curiously in the direction of the window, attention drawn by the bird's whistle, and then faced her again. "Thank you."

"Don't mention it," she said dismissively. She folded her arms, adding a second physical barrier to the one formed by her yet unpacked bags, which lay between them on the floor. She saw no need to be polite, so she phrased her next question baldly. "What're you doing here? You'd better be researching a new tour package."

"No."

She tried again. "Vacation?"

He laughed softly, as though the thought wouldn't have occurred to him. "No."

She pressed her fists against her ribs in impatience. If he continued to be this talkative, they'd be here all night. Not exactly what she had in mind for her first evening in France. She'd been thinking more along the lines of dinner at a bistro around the corner, maybe a show. As far as she was concerned, he could do whatever he'd come to do and then get the hell out. "Well, what then?"

"I came to see you."

That was a laugh, if she ever heard one. "Why? Is more money missing from Wanderlust? Cufflinks upped and gone from your bedside table?"

He winced. "No, nothing like that. I needed to see you."

"And you just happened to be passing by a hotel that I happened to be staying in?" She couldn't keep the scorn and distrust off her face; she didn't even try. "Come on. You can take me for lots of things, but don't take me for a fool."

He shook his head emphatically. "No, I swear, I'm not…" He sighed and ran his fingers through his hair. The gesture drew her eyes to the fourth finger of his left hand. The familiar gold band was gone. It its place was a pale shadow that mesmerized her like a saint's halo.

"You want to sit down?" he suggested.

The two cute little damask-covered chairs in the corner of the room were placed way too close together. Too cozy. If she sat with him, her knee might brush his.

"No."

He didn't insist. He stood on his two feet and answered her question as baldly as she'd asked it. "I'm here because I knew you'd be here."

She squinted at him in suspicion. "And how, pray tell, did you know I'd be here?"

Wearily, he confessed. "I own a travel agency. It's not all that hard to know when someone's booking a plane ticket or a hotel room, when you're linked up to the network and know the right people."

Her gasp was audible. Her curse even more so. "You've been spying on me?"

"I've been…I just wanted to be alerted if you tried to leave Santa Amata."

The bags between them proved to be no barrier at all. Kendra leaped over them, grabbed hold of Trey's shirt sleeve, and began dragging him toward the door. "Out."

He resisted. "Please, no."

Finding him near immovable, she pointed at the locked door and shrieked, "Out! Get out! You're a creep and a pig and a…a…Peeping Tom! I can't believe you once had the nerve to accuse *me* of stalking *you!*"

"At least let me explain."

She was way too mad for an explanation. "You got three seconds…"

"I know I was wrong."

"…to get out,…"

"It was dumb, I know. But I didn't do it for the reasons you think…."

"…or I start screaming."

"I didn't follow you here to persecute you."

"One…!"

"It's not about money, or anything like that…."

"Two…!" She counted off on her fingers, but to her chagrin, he still wasn't showing any signs of moving toward the door. What if she got to three and he didn't budge?

"It was a stupid thing to do,…"

"I'm going to scream, Trey. Honest I will. I'm going to yell for the cops." "Police" meant "police" in any language, right?

"…but love makes men do really stupid things sometimes."

"Three…*what?*" She'd filled her lungs with enough air for a loud, hearty B-movie-horror-heroine scream, and then choked on it.

He gave her a ghost of a smile. "You heard right."

She'd heard right, sure, but she wasn't buying it for a second. "Right. You came here…"

"Because I needed to see you."

"Ah. You crossed the Atlantic to see me, when for the past few months I've been twenty minutes away by car? Very funny, Trey. I'm laughing, see?" She bared her teeth at him. "Good. Joke over. Go away and leave me be."

"It's not a joke. Believe me, I feel like a jerk. But I've had a truly horrible time. Letting my anger consume me. Being hurt, and hating you for it."

"Charming."

"It literally ate me up. I could barely work, barely eat, barely sleep. I was in no condition to come after you."

She looked at his eyes again. Not into them, but around them. She could see the fine lines that radiated from them that hadn't been there before. There were lines around his mouth, too and they weren't from smiling. She felt as though she'd fallen through a time tunnel and met him on the other side. "You treat me like Typhoid Mary all the time I'm living in your own city, yet when your little spy network told you I was flying to Paris you came after me? That sound sane to you?"

"It sounds crazy as a June bug. But I panicked. You booked a one-way ticket. I got scared. I thought you were leaving for good."

"I booked a one-way because I'm here on business, and I didn't know how long that would take." She noticed she was still holding on to his shirtsleeve, and she let it go as if it burned.

"You got a job with another travel agency?"

"No, I didn't." Part of her was bursting to tell him all about her new position, to make him proud of her. The other part didn't give a damn whether he was impressed or not. She didn't need his admiration. "Long story. Not the time for it."

Getting into that would mean more time in his presence, and she was too weak to hold up much longer. Let him talk, she pleaded silently, and then let him go. He'd mentioned love, and then swung right around back to hate. She couldn't take this seesawing. Her heart couldn't take it. So, please, just let him go.

"I thought that if you upped and left, you might disappear into thin air, and then I'd never get the chance to see you again."

"So you followed me across an *ocean?*"

He looked as though he hadn't quite thought of it that way until now. "And across a city. I've got a room downstairs."

"Maybe you should go back to it."

He shook his head in an emphatic no. "Not until I get what I came for."

The burning lump in her throat made it hard to ask her question. "What'd you come for?"

"You."

His face was so sober, so tense, so full of strain, that she wanted to reach up and caress his creased, tired cheek. But she was afraid such a gesture would be the point of no return, and her weakness would be exposed. So instead, she stared down at the fallen suitcase. "Don't do this to me, Trey."

"Do what?"

"Don't come here and fill my head with rubbish. You're tired and grieving. You lost your mother. That alone would make a man weak. You're lonely and you don't know what you're feeling. You're hoping for a connection, that's all."

"I'm grieving, yes, and I'll probably grieve for a long time. But that doesn't mean I can't recognize love when I see it."

"You didn't recognize it the last time," she pointed out cruelly. "When I was offering it to you."

Shame dulled his eyes even more. "I'm so sorry…."

She had to get away. She darted around him, hoping he wouldn't reach out and try to pull her to him as she passed, and ran onto what was quite possibly the tiniest balcony in Europe. Bad move. With her back against the iron railing, she was trapped.

He stood in the doorway. "Is there any of that left?"

She pretended not to get him. "Is there any what left?"

"Love. For me."

Loads, her heart was yelling. Loads and loads and loads. "Why? What's the point? You hate me."

"I thought I did. Who I really hated was myself—for letting you in."

"Well, you don't trust me. You called me a con artist. You damn near called me a whore."

He squeezed his eyes closed. "Forgive me." Behind him, the little blue bird sang on, oblivious.

"It's not a matter of forgiving. It doesn't make sense. You didn't trust me then. What's to say you'll trust me in the future?"

"That's all over." He waved it away. "I've forgotten all that."

"Well, I haven't!" Her voice was loud enough for a pedestrian below to turn his face toward them. She lowered it. "I pleaded with you to believe me. In the name of love, I begged you. All you had to do was listen. But you were *so* stingy with your trust."

He leaned wearily against the doorjamb. "Listen, Kendra. Let me tell you something. In the last few months since we were together, I've thought about nothing but you, and me, and what happened. And Lord knows, I've had time to think. I haven't had a restful night's sleep since. And the only conclusion I can come to is that it was never about trusting you or not trusting you. That was just an excuse. In spite of everything I said, I was still feeling guilty about cheating on Ashia."

He paused as though he expected her to interrupt him. She didn't. He went on. "There was still a part of me that felt I shouldn't be doing this, but I was falling in love with you so fast that I was starting to panic. Then I came in that morning and found the report from my auditors, and bang, I had the perfect excuse. I saw an out and I took it."

"And nearly destroyed me in the process."

"I am so, so sorry. Believe me, if it takes twenty years for me to make it up to you, I'll do it."

"You don't have twenty years."

"Then give me twenty days."

"To do what? You've already taken up twenty minutes of my time that you don't deserve." It was a brutal response. She thought his pained reaction would bring her pleasure, but it didn't.

"I mean it, just give me three weeks to woo you properly. To prove to you I'm not the bastard you think I am."

She must be suffering from jet lag, because all this was beginning to sound good. Try as she might, she couldn't sustain her anger at the level she would have preferred. The level that would keep her safe from him. She made one last-ditch effort. "Why would I want to do that?"

"Because I know you still love me," he responded, without a trace of arrogance.

Denial was right there, balanced on her tongue, but she couldn't let the words past her lips. Instead, she asked, "How d'you…"

He stepped onto the way-too-small balcony, so he was close enough to touch—if she wanted to. And she wanted to, but didn't dare. "If there's one thing I learned from losing Ashia," he explained, "it's that love never dies. It prevails over death. It can prevail over meanness, cruelty, fear and anger, everything I threw at you to keep you away. I know it can, because it's stronger."

Denying that she loved him would have been a sacrilege. Throwing something precious and God-given back up to Heaven where it had been forged. So she tried to reason with him. "It'll never work."

"It can. It will. Even my mother thought—" He stopped, and something flickered across his face.

"Your mother?" She'd been burdened by the certainty that Marlene had died with nothing but disdain and recrimination for Kendra and the trick she'd played on her. She'd been sure Trey's mother had refused to speak of her ever again. But Marlene had said something about them? What?

"My mother knew I loved you before I did. She thought this was right for us, even though we couldn't see it ourselves. She thought I belonged in your life."

News that good couldn't possibly be true. "How d'you know that?"

"Because, ever since I told her I broke up with you, I was in the doghouse. She called me every kind of fool. Told me the family brains must have skipped a generation, because I was a blamed idiot for letting you go. I tried not to listen, but I knew she was right." His smile was full of warm memories, tinged with loss.

That sounded like something Marlene would say. "Your Mom thought that, even though we…*I* lied to her? Over and over…?"

"She forgave you, Kendra. She understood." He fished in the pocket of his pants. "I almost forgot." He withdrew a small, folded, peach-colored envelope that crinkled as he handed it over.

She held her hand out gingerly. "What's this?"

"She made me promise to deliver this to you. *Deliver* it, she insisted. She told me she'd have my head if she ever found out I'd mailed it."

Kendra turned it over, once, twice; elated, curious, flat-out scared. On the front, her name was written in a determined but feminine hand. The back was sealed with a round sticker embossed with a capital M. The precious words inside made it weighty. She slid her finger under the seal, but Trey stopped her with a hand.

"Not now," he said. "Tomorrow."

She paused, finger still stuck in the envelope. "Why?"

"Know in your heart that there's nothing in there but my mother's love. Read it when you're alone, so you can absorb everything she had to say to you. But not tonight. We have unfinished business." He took the envelope from her and carefully set it down on a table the size of an upturned plant pot.

She looked longingly at the letter; but he was right. There was something bigger here, waiting. He was waiting. Everything in her made her want to go to him, but she held back, needing reassurance. "You're here because your mother wanted you to be with me?"

He shook his head emphatically, vigorously enough to force even the suggestion of such a thing out of it. "No, no, sweet. I'm here because *I* want to be with you. My mom can be— could be—a bully, but bless her, she didn't make this decision for me. I did." He waited.

She thought about it. At least her mind still had to think. Her body had already made a decision, and was tilting so far forward it was a wonder she didn't hit the deck.

But he waited silently. Humbly. Trying not to rush her. Then, as the seconds stretching between them grew longer and longer, his body did as hers longed to do. He moved closer again. She had two choices: it was over the balcony or into his arms. She figured his arms were the better choice. She stumbled into them and was immediately enfolded. He wrapped himself around her, pulling her so close she had to sustain herself with little breaths, tiny sips of air. He was trembling.

"Thank you," he said.

"I missed you."

"I missed you every day. I thought about you every day. Every night. So many times I wanted to call you. Or come see you."

"Why didn't you?"

"I was too ashamed. I was afraid to face the reflection of myself I'd see in your eyes." He looked down at her as she tilted her face up to him. "I was afraid of exactly the reflection of me I saw in you when you opened that door." She felt his belly vibrate as he laughed softly. "The *second* time you opened the door."

Then he was serious again. "I promise you, I will never put that look there again." Then, on that tiny balcony overlooking an ancient street, with the Parisian skies darkening above, he kissed her. It was the kind of kiss that washed away sorrow and pain and made everything new again. When it was over, he took her hand. "Come."

He led her inside, sat on the big willow bed and lifted her onto his lap. She curled her arms around his neck, whispering his name against his skin. "I love you," she told him. "I couldn't stop. I wanted to, but I couldn't." Joy made her light-headed. It was a glow that filled her, seeped into him and spread throughout the room. She kissed him, pressing her hands against his chest and feeling ribs where powerful muscle had once been. She'd have to feed him up. The thought made her laugh against his lips.

"What?" he whispered, curious, but not enough to interrupt their kiss.

"Mmmph," she answered, which she hoped he'd correctly interpret to mean "Nothing."

When they were all kissed out, she pulled her blood-flushed lips away from his and looked up to find him beaming down at her. She had to share her wonderment, "I feel so full!"

"Full?"

"Not hungry, not yearning. Not longing for anything anymore. I don't feel like there's a space inside me that I need to fill up with cupcakes and candy. And I don't feel like I need to cover myself in fancy clothes to make myself pretty. I feel…wonderful."

"You *are* wonderful." The light she'd come to love so much was back in his eyes; just a glimmer of it, but she knew that, in time, it would grow again. He added, with a sly smile, "And I can tell you I'm thinking of a space inside you that I'm dying to fill, and you certainly don't need clothes for that."

Normally, a comment like that would merit a sharp rap across the knuckles, at least, but she was overflowing with love and hope, and, besides, they were in *Paris*…naughtiness was not only forgiven, it was encouraged. She took his hand and pressed her lips against the untanned skin that encircled his ring finger.

"You are, huh?" She was smiling hugely, wickedly.

"Yep. So I hope you haven't made any plans for the night."

"If I made any, they're pretty much done for now." What he was proposing was a whole lot more exciting than dinner at a bistro and a show, anyway.

"Good. And tomorrow…"

"Tomorrow?"

He said in all seriousness, "I know you're here to work, but you're just going to have to do whatever it is you came to do with me stuck to you like Velcro. I haven't got a whole lot of time, and the clock's ticking."

She frowned, puzzled. "Why haven't you got a whole lot of time?"

He shifted her off his lap and onto her back, high up on the bed so he could stretch himself out upon her, so they could be face-to-face when he answered. "I asked you for twenty days for me to prove to you that I'm worthy—"

"But you *are*—"

He didn't let her finish. "I'm not going to waste a second of it. I'm going to spend the next three weeks of my life convincing you that this is no mistake. This is real. When I'm done with you, Kendra, Kate, Natalie, whatever, I don't care, you'll know without a fraction of a doubt that I love you. When I'm done with you, sweet, you'll know that the Trey you fell in love with was only half the man I intend to become again." He slipped one hand into the opening of her blouse and cupped her breast.

Joy filled her like helium, lifting her up, making her dizzy. If his body, so intimately connected with hers as he lay upon her, wasn't so heavy, she'd have floated clear up to the ceiling. Whatever he was planning on doing to her, however he was planning on showing his love, she knew it was going to be better than anything she'd dreamed of in all those lonely months without him. Better than anything that had gone before. And whatever he was planning to do to her, she knew she would explode if he didn't start right now.

She glanced at the bedside clock, and then back at him. There was a devil in his eyes. "Clock's ticking," she observed.

"Sure is." The buttons on her blouse were no barrier to him. "Time's wasting."

"It waits for no man." The catch on her bra popped loose.

She grasped the wrist of the hand that was *not* wreaking

havoc with her senses, and sucked his thumb into her mouth, raking the skin with her teeth. "Then I guess you'd better get busy," she managed to say, although her mouth was full.

He got busy. And he knew he was right where he wanted to be.

HOLLINGTON HOMECOMING

*Where old friends reunite…
and new passions take flight.*

Book #1 by Sandra Kitt
RSVP WITH LOVE
September 2009

Book #2 by Jacquelin Thomas
TEACH ME TONIGHT
October 2009

Book #3 by Pamela Yaye
PASSION OVERTIME
November 2009

Book #4 by Adrianne Byrd
TENDER TO HIS TOUCH
December 2009

Ten Years. Eight Grads. One weekend.
The homecoming of a lifetime.

www.kimanipress.com
www.myspace.com/kimanipress

KPHHSP

REQUEST YOUR FREE BOOKS!

2 FREE NOVELS
PLUS 2 FREE GIFTS!

KIMANI™
ROMANCE

Love's ultimate destination!

KROM09

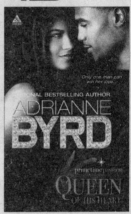

HELP CELEBRATE
ARABESQUE'S
15TH ANNIVERSARY!

2009 marks Arabesque's 15th anniversary!

Help us celebrate by telling us about your most special memories and moments with Arabesque books. Entries will be judged by the Arabesque Anniversary Committee based on which are the most touching and well written. Fifteen lucky winners will receive as a prize a full-grain leather duffel bag with the Arabesque anniversary logo.

VISIT **WWW.MYSPACE.COM/KIMANIPRESS**
FOR THE COMPLETE OFFICIAL RULES